TOMORROW IS FOREVER

A NOVEL

DOLORES DURANDO

This book is a work of fiction. Names, characters, places, and incidents are products of the author's imagination or are used fictitiously. Any resemblance of actual events or locales or persons, living or dead, is entirely incidental.

ISBN 979-8-9866994-5-5

Cover and book design by Barbara Holiday
Published by N8tive Run Press, a subsidiary of
N8tive Run Enterprises, 5007 Laurel Avenue, Grants Pass, OR 97527

DEDICATION

For my beloved son, Bill, and his true love, Cathy,
without whom I never would have
finished this love story.

ACKNOWLEDGEMENT

Again and again, my deepest appreciation for
my loyal, patient, indispensable editor,
Barbara Holiday,
who endeavors to make me better
and forgives me my spelling.

CHAPTER 1

It was 1964, and I was crowding seventy-six.

It was the time of day I loved the most. The sun barely up, the soft shadow of the wisteria vine against the corner of the big window, then scrambling over the rooftop as though it could hear the click-click of my pruning shears.

I sat in my favorite chair watching through the window the raucous blue jays quarreling and the occasional blue feather as it floated downward. Then my glance shifted to the colorful tulips and the crocuses that defied the patches of snow to make their dramatic entrance against the coming green of the lawn. I could almost feel the push of the buds on the apple tree as they waited impatiently for the sun.

There was a slight chill in the air this morning, so I built a little fire in the old woodstove. The warmth seemed to enhance the fragrance of my coffee. I poured another cup, leaned back in my chair, and reveled in the peace and joy of the serenity of the countryside.

Closing my eyes, I daydreamed and reminisced about this house in which I had been born and raised over seventy-five years ago.

Rousing myself, my drowsy gaze stared through the early morning mist. I could vaguely see the cupola, now tilted, on the faded red barn, the outline of the neighboring old house—a ten-minute walk down a dirt road and even shorter if I walked the path through the pasture. A well-to-do doctor from our nearest town, Cedar Heights, had bought the forty acres adjoining ours when I was still in grade school, and Dad had built the elaborate fourteen-stall barn with a ten-foot-high cupola visible for miles around. It housed the doctor's hobby: purebred Arabians.

Dad called it "Halstad's Folly."

The house was truly beautiful with its ornate cornices, leaded-glass windows and wraparound veranda, but my mother sniffed at the fancy house and the doctor's fancy wife, who kept her friends in town and made no secret of her distaste for country living.

I went to grade school with the doctor's two sons. I chuckled to myself as I remembered James, the youngest, who put the snake in my desk, and Charles, who called me "Red" and always pulled the ribbons that held my pigtails secure.

When spring arrived eight years later, the doctor's wife left, taking James with her. The doctor sold his horses, boarded up the house and closed his practice, and sent Charles to an expensive boarding school. The community had to take their medical needs to Portland, sixty miles away.

As the years slipped by, we continued to farm, but not seriously. Since Dad was a contractor he worked in the surrounding area. As I grew older I tended the chickens, milked the two cows, cared for the few sheep that kept the grass down. Mother had a garden that she loved and baked apple pies that won first place at the county fair. She died the year I graduated from high school. Dad was inconsolable and joined her the following year.

I found myself alone in our little two-bedroom house and it seemed too big. My mother and father had planned that college was in the future for me, but now that seemed so far away.

Then I was asked to teach in the little rural one-room schoolhouse. Although I had only a high-school diploma, the school board was happy to have me since teachers were hard to come by and didn't stay long in the country.

But coming home from school every night to correct papers became tiresome. I had lost contact with my friends from high school, who had mostly moved on after graduation, and it was lonely on the farm. I knew there had to be something more, but what?

Appraising myself one day, I looked in the mirror and saw a mop of red hair—almost untamable—the nice straight nose of my mother, and the heavily lashed gray-green eyes of my father. I stepped on the scale—a hundred and thirty pounds. Standing against the doorjamb, where Mother had marked my height for over twelve years, I added a few inches to it to mark my current height of five feet four.

I decided to terminate my teaching career after the spring semester, when I boarded up the little house, locked the barn where Dad's old truck stood rusting, his sweat-stained hat still resting on the seat, and moved to Portland, where the bright lights were. I felt very adventuresome and made new friends. Among them was a laughing brown-eyed boy with long hair and tie-dyed clothes with whom I fell madly in love. He said wanted to marry me, then sell the farm so that he could travel and "find himself." Heartbroken, I sent him on his way, swearing never to be so foolish again.

Less than a year later, it was a quiet, soft-spoken and well-dressed man who danced with such grace and swore I was the center of his universe.

But an accidental encounter with my man in the produce department of a large market proved otherwise. A little girl lifted her arms, crying "Daddy," and a very pregnant lady was by his side.

My small-town illusions thus shattered, I decided to enroll in a prestigious nursing school. The years that followed were a challenge, but I earned the white cap that declared me to be a medical professional.

Then, after years in the big city, a subtle change began to haunt me. I lay awake nights; interest in my chosen field wavering. Something was nagging me. My hands kept busy but could not compete with the turmoil that rampaged through my every waking moment. In this beautiful city with thousands of people, I felt isolated.

Like a bolt from the blue, it came to me in the middle of the night—I was lonesome for my home, for my mountain, for my kind of people. So, two weeks later, I was charge nurse at Cedar Heights Community Hospital.

I have a framed certificate on my wall that reads, "Emma Lindstrom, charge nurse, has given twenty years of valuable service to the pediatric division of the Community Hospital, Cedar Heights, Oregon." It was my honest opinion that I had helped deliver three quarters of the county's population.

My little house, built solidly on the doorstep of Mount Grayback, now sported a new roof, plumbing, and other niceties. The big house, a short walk down the road, had not fared so well. I closed my eyes, visualizing the house that once had been so beautiful, but was now slumped on its crumbling foundation, desolate and forlorn, its aura of loneliness almost human.

A sagging gate hung by a twisted hinge clinging to a rotting post, suggesting that once there had been a fence.

I awoke with a start from my reverie, found that my coffee had grown cold and I hadn't even had a piece of toast! Surely I hadn't dozed off—there are two flats of pansies waiting for their final destination along the walk and one corner of the lawn needs to be reseeded where the moles have certainly made a mess. A good cat that hunts for its dinner would be a joy!

Hurriedly pulling on my jeans, I searched for my shirt and sweater while my coffee boiled over in the microwave and black smoke drifted from the toaster. A dozen things to do. Breakfast can wait.

My yard is my passion—every blade of grass has been trimmed to perfection. With trowel in hand, I placed the first pansy.

The irises will make their usual springtime debut around the driveway; my peonies promised their exquisite blooms soon; the hostas beneath the apple tree that stands at the kitchen window are early.

I love this land—my peaceful refuge in this noisy, busy world.

Days later, while working in my garden with my breakfast hardly settled, the loud sound of a big truck broke the morning stillness. I watched it slow, then turn into the weed-covered driveway and stop in front of the old house. Another truck followed soon thereafter. Consumed with curiosity, I pocketed my gardening gloves and walked the shortcut through the pasture.

Passing the big truck, I read the logo on the door: M.A. Jorgenson Construction—Design, Build, Remodel. Satisfaction guaranteed. 541-660-4132.

Oh, no, I thought, they're going to tear down the old house.

A feeling of nostalgia swept over me. I identified with this house. The two men who were walking about, talking, laughing, taking notes as they appraised the house, were startled to see a gray-haired old lady leaning against a truck with tears in her eyes. In a trembling voice, I introduced myself.

"How sad I am to see the old house demolished. You can't imagine how beautiful it once was."

The man patted my shoulder. "Don't be sad, lady. The house is not coming down. It will be more beautiful than before when we're finished with it, and that will be sooner than you think. A generous bonus if it's done in two months to the satisfaction of this gentleman in Florida."

"Florida," I exclaimed. "That's a long way from Oregon. May I ask who my new neighbor will be?"

"His name is Halstad. He called from Florida to make arrangements. Said it was the family's old home." The man smiled and tipped his hat. "Lady, if I'm gonna collect that bonus, I gotta get started."

Walking home comforted by the builder's promise, I realized that the man in Florida must be one of the Halstad boys or, most likely, their kids or grandchildren. Oh, dear. That will probably mean parties every night, cars coming and going, spewing dust to high heaven. My peace of mind was suddenly gone. In fact, I made myself miserable thinking about it. I hope they stay on their own side of the fence was my last thought before sleep closed my eyes.

A couple of days later, a whole army of men and equipment swarmed over the house like a disturbed beehive. My head ached with the clutter and bang that made the air heavy with dust. Gone was my joy in the gardens.

The new foundation took over a week to complete, and now the old house had gotten off her knees and stood proud. The workmen scurried about. From the sagging roof the remaining shingles flew through the air to join the exhaust fumes from the heavy equipment. By the end of the month, the house began to take shape. The second month went slower—the finish work was exacting.

The contractor started to sweat. Now, with just weeks to go, it started to come together. A fine new fence with an impressive metal gate. A newly seeded lawn. Even the cupola on the barn stood erect.

"I believe that man is going to get his bonus," I laughed. "He's earned it."

When the workmen finished, they gathered up their equipment and left. The house was perhaps more beautiful than before—just as the contractor had promised.

Walking through the pasture and up the new steps that led to a rebuilt veranda, I peered through the windows and saw shiny new floors and lovely cabinetry. The house was painted the original white, and green shutters now framed the windows—a perfect touch.

I wondered if that "horde of Halstads," as I referred to them in my mind, would appreciate the beauty of it and when they would arrive.

Thinking it would be a neighborly gesture to at least greet them with a casserole, I forced that thought out of my mind. My mean little heart didn't want to be neighborly. My only desire was peace and quiet in my own little garden in my own little world.

Now spring has sprung, my radishes are up, and a very visible row of corn is poking up through the dirt. I could almost taste that buttered sweet corn. And the strawberries— their modest white flowers are no competition for the pansies and irises in full bloom.

The sun had been hot, and I was tired and sweaty and obsessing with the idea of a long cold shower, a cup of tea and perhaps a sandwich, and enjoying the rest of the day with the newspaper.

The tea hadn't cooled before the quiet hum of an approaching car sounded. Pulling the curtain back at the kitchen window, I watched as a big black car drove slowly up the driveway. A tall, slightly stooped man, with more white in his hair than gray, stepped out and opened the gate, then stopped at the house. He carried a suitcase and a bag that I assumed contained groceries.

He walked slowly, pausing on the veranda steps as though he was exhausted, then crossed to the entrance, fumbled for a moment with a key, then opened the door, closing it behind him immediately.

Aha, it occurred to me, they've sent Grandpa on ahead.

My mind did the arithmetic—which one of the boys could it be? Boys? Charles was two grades ahead of me in school; he must be getting close to eighty now.

I felt ashamed. It wouldn't have hurt me a bit to have made that casserole.

CHAPTER 2

All was quiet at the Halstad place. Of course, I saw the old man walking about, and very briskly, too, for a man of his age. He seemed to spend a lot of time in the barn. A black thought crept into my mind: He wouldn't dare be following his father's footsteps and bring in horses. Then another thought followed: Surely that could never happen—not at his age.

Wednesday was my baking day. I'd starve before I'd eat pitiful store-bought bread—may as well make an apple pie while the bread rises. I mixed the dough and set it on the back of the stove. Then my attention turned to the pie and shortly it was in the oven. Soon the aroma of that pie made even my mouth water. After checking the bread dough, and rolling it out on a floured board, kneading and turning it every which way, I visualized the strawberry jam waiting.

Now the pie was browned to perfection, out of the oven, and set aside to cool.

My mind ran ahead as I worked, and I realized that I was going to be done earlier than anticipated. Maybe I'll have time to tie those tomatoes up, check the lawn mower, and maybe…

There was a soft knock on the door.

Wiping my floury hands on my apron, I opened the door to Charles Halstad and his wide smile.

"Hello, Red." He held out his hand, and added, "Well, I guess it's not red anymore, but it's still curly. Remember me?"

"Of course, Charles. I'm not going blind in my old age!"

He laughed and I saw that his teeth were his own.

"Old age?" You're at least two years younger than I am and I'm not old yet. May I come in? We're neighbors again as you've probably noticed."

"Come in." What else could I say? No, I'm planning to work in my garden? But as he stood there smiling and waiting in an immaculate white shirt, I held the door wide and said, "Come in and have a cup of coffee."

"Ah, that would be great. I haven't been able to make a decent cup. What is that wonderful smell?" He sniffed appreciatively. "I remember your mother always made apple pie. Oh, there it is. I'll bet it would taste as good as it looks."

I placed a steaming cup of coffee before him. "Cream? Sugar?"

"Oh, no. This is too good to spoil. Won't you join me?"

"You'll have to give me a moment. This bread dough needs to be pushed down."

"Homemade bread? How wonderful! I wonder if it will be as good as the pie."

Knowing when I'm whipped, I said a bit sarcastically, "Could I force a piece of that pie on you? You wouldn't be offended?"

He grinned. "Now, Red, what makes you think I'd be offended? If you're worried about it, I'd be happy to test it for you."

I gave him a fork and a napkin, cut one third of that pie and gave it to him on a dinner plate. That pie disappeared so quickly, for a moment I doubted that I had actually cut it.

"I'd be delighted to test for you anytime, just call," he laughed.

With my back to him, I continued to punish that dough and asked over my shoulder, "When is the rest of your family going to join you?"

"I am the family. My wife died fifty years ago and I never remarried. I'm all that's left of the Halstads."

The loneliness in his voice made me sorry about my question.

The dough finished for the moment, I refilled his cup, poured one for myself and joined him.

"That house is awfully big for one man."

"I'm going to be too busy to notice," he answered. "I'm retired and going to start a new career. I'm going to be a farmer."

Wordlessly, I looked at him in amazement. White starched shirt, obviously expensive tailored trousers, shoes not made for barn work. Choking on my laughter, I asked, "What was your profession?"

"I worked in a bank."

"That must have been monotonous standing behind a cage for hours."

"I wouldn't know about that. I was the president of Tampa First National for twenty years."

I was absolutely dumb struck. For the first time, I really looked at him, a few feet of table between us. Tall and spare, his white hair barbered to perfection, elegantly dressed. Beautiful hands that had never known a callus, now folding a napkin. I couldn't imagine him milking a cow or shoveling manure! He looked like a bank president. And his eyes were so…so blue.

Well, he might be Mr. Halstad in Florida, but he was just plain Charles to me. I wished he'd go home. My outside work waited, but he was in a talkative mood.

"I've been reading a good book," he said. "Lots of good information in the *Farmers' Almanac*. A farm needs livestock—cows for my own cream and butter, chickens for fresh eggs, and a big tractor."

My worst fears were coming true. I looked at my cup, not wanting him to see the look in my eyes.

"I've already bought the tractor. Gets delivered tomorrow."

The thought occurred to me that if he enjoys playing farmer with that tractor, maybe he'll forget the cows and chickens.

"I'm probably taking too much of your time, Red." He lay his napkin down and stood. "Thank you for that wonderful pie."

CHAPTER 3

My life seemed to have done a turnaround. In the bat of an eye, my plans would change. There was no time to spend in my garden and it was easy to see the weeds—something unknown of in the past. The roses never did get properly pruned, nor did that kitchen screen get replaced.

Almost every day Charles had a problem. His tractor was a menace. The first day he drove it, he got the gas pedal confused with reverse. His tractor raced over the riding lawnmower, with pieces flying in all directions.

Hearing the sounds so close, I ran out shrieking, "Turn it off! Turn it off!" But all he heard was "Turn" and I ran for my life.

Finally he found the brakes. Looking back, he saw that he had run down about twenty yards of fence and most of it was wrapped around his wheels.

He crawled down, pale-faced, and said in a voice I hadn't heard before, "This farming is a hazardous business," and wiped his sweaty face.

"Charles," I said, "you should have kept your day job."

"Maybe I should start another line of work, perhaps a dairy."

"Don't you dare bring any animals here—look at your fences! You are not a farmer."

"Well, I'm going to the auction tomorrow. Surely I can just look? Call me when the bread is ready."

He walked me to my door. As he turned to say good-bye, he pulled a spotless white handkerchief from his pocket, leaned down and brushed my cheek.

"Flour," he said.

I punched that dough down so hard Mohammed Ali would have come in a poor second.

It was the worst loaf of bread that oven had ever known.

Several days passed. All was quiet at the Halstad place, so my world was peaceful too. And now my garden was without a weed. I kept an eye on the big house, saw the smoke floating above, and surmised that Charles had survived his own cooking and knew how to build a fire. We waved to each other when we both happened to be out at the same time.

Then, on a Wednesday, he followed the wave to his side of the fence and teased, "Hey, Red, isn't that bread done yet?"

As a matter of fact, I had just pulled it out of the oven and it was still cooling.

"He must have a nose like a bloodhound," I muttered to myself while stomping back to the house. I had wanted to fertilize the roses, but who could ignore that pitiful plea? The roses would have to wait.

As I put the coffee on, Charles was at the door. Half a loaf, spread liberally with my strawberry jam, disappeared in the twinkling of an eye, along with three eggs over easy.

I leaned over and wiped a strawberry smear from that white shirt with the monogram on the cuff.

My face flushed as he said, "Thank you, Red, and thank you for this wonderful breakfast."

Hoping he knew a bribe when he saw one, the rest of the loaf went home with him and with it a fresh jar of jam. With his money, he could buy a bakery.

This is absolutely the last time—I'm not going to continue with this nonsense. Then a thought intruded: But it was nice to sit across the table from an intelligent man…and his eyes, under those white eyebrows, were so, so, so blue.

Later he drove off—in his black Cadillac that wasn't so black anymore, more an off-color gray. The road was getting dry; the spring rains no longer kept the car shiny.

Upon his return, I could hear the cackling of the chickens before he turned into the driveway. From the trunk of his car, he unloaded two crates with feathered heads pushing through the slats. An indignant crow came from the back seat.

Charles stopped when he saw me.

"Red," he shouted joyously. "Come see! Ten hens and a rooster."

I admired the hens, but the rooster turned a baleful eye to me and, with one foot through the slot, showed me a spur at least three inches long—sharp and pointed in my direction. He looked like trouble.

Charles's face was beaming. "Fresh eggs, Red."

Ever practical, I asked, "Where are you going to keep them?"

"Oh, that's no problem. They've got forty acres to scratch around on."

"Charles," I said reluctantly, for I hated to rain on his parade, "these hens will hide their nests everywhere. You will be fortunate to get enough eggs for breakfast. And the fox that lives here will surely thin those hens overnight."

He looked so disappointed that I added, "You need a fenced yard and roosts and nesting boxes."

"I thought they'd look so pretty in the yard."

"They will look just as pretty in a pen and you'll have eggs. Better keep them in the barn until you can have a pen built."

Two days later a carpenter had constructed a henhouse with all the accessories that was almost as big as my house.

Who knows how they captured those chickens and moved them to the pen, but on hearing the truck burn rubber on that new driveway, I figured it hadn't been easy.

It wasn't even daylight when I was awakened by a sound similar to that of a train as it approached a crossing. The rooster's good-morning greeting and all the ones that followed made me yearn for a hatchet. In my mind's eye, I could see my bedroom was a straight line from that chicken coop and downwind. Every morning without fail, I lay awake, waiting for that rooster to crow.

After a week that pushed me to near madness, I walked over to the big house, prepared to voice a strong complaint. Charles was in the chicken pen gathering eggs. Proudly he showed me the half-full container. He couldn't have been more thrilled had they been diamonds. He looked fondly at the hens gathered around us.

"Aren't they beautiful? Look how the feathers shine. The man said they were a rare breed—white leghorns. You know, Dad always wanted me to be in the banking business, but I've always wanted to be a farmer. I've never forgotten this place."

I wanted to say, "Ten chickens never made a farm, Charles," but restrained myself. Lack of sleep had certainly put me in a witchy mood.

"Now, about that rooster, Charles," and I pointed to that bird that had never taken his beady eyes off me. He strolled back and forth in front of me, dragging a wing, obviously a challenge.

"Yes," Charles said, "isn't he magnificent? You should hear him crow."

He turned to investigate another nest and I casually reached for a rake that was leaning against the fence.

Suddenly the rooster flew up with both feet extended, and I saw the sun glint on the long-pointed spurs. The rake caught him in midair and he dropped as though he didn't have a bone in his body. Charles was horrified.

"Red, why did you do that? He only wanted to play. You shouldn't have done that. Now we'll never have any eggs."

"Charles, I'm sorry to have killed your rooster," I lied, and added, "You know you don't need a rooster to get eggs."

He looked at me bewildered. "Why, Red," he said, "surely you must know what it takes to procreate."

"Guess you didn't have much time for biology in the banking business," I snapped.

With some ice in his voice, he said, "Red, you've been in the country too long. I thought it was common knowledge that it takes two."

This was getting pretty close to fisticuffs.

I nudged the rooster with the rake and said, "I'll bury this damned rooster since I killed him."

As if those were the magic words, that bird wobbled to his feet and squawked out the imitation of a crow.

That rooster held a grudge. Every morning and throughout the day he stood on a post facing my house and avenged himself. The earth trembled.

Then one day only a few feathers lay about the post. Apparently, a chicken hawk had fallen in love with that musical bird and wanted that rooster for his own.

The hens never noticed. Peace was restored.

CHAPTER 4

How wonderful to sleep in these last mornings. That rooster had blasted me awake for a week.

Holding firm to my resolution to stop this Wednesday-morning breakfast thing, I planned to be up early, have a quick cup of coffee, and be busy outside if Charles came over.

Quickly tying my old barn boots and reaching for my sweater, I glimpsed him taking the shortcut. His white hair was a little shaggy now, made him look almost boyish. Walking quickly, his back was as straight as a man half his age. Where had the stoop gone? I laughed to see him in striped bib overalls, the hem somewhere above his ankles.

Opening the door before he could knock, I told him that breakfast was over and a window box was already under construction.

"Yes," he said. "I'm going to be busy most of the day too."

With that, he handed me a bucket that held big brown eggs.

"Charles," I sniped in exaggerated surprise. "Have you been to the market so early?"

Not missing my barb, he said stiffly, "Hardly. These are from my hens, of course."

I wasn't going to let him off easy, him and his procreation.

"You mean to tell me that those hens have done this all by themselves? Guess they don't know about procreation."

He looked me right in the eye and spoke quietly. "Red, you are a most aggravating woman."

My lame retort came quickly. "Charles, didn't they have those overalls in your size?"

Watching his car go down the driveway, an inexplicable feeling swept over me. My arthritis was probably acting up again.

Late in the afternoon the sound of his car was muffled by a large truck pulling a trailer of sorts that parked by the barn. I couldn't see through the trees, but could hear a lot of banging about and words that Charles wouldn't use. Then the truck and trailer rattled back down the driveway.

I had worked most of the day on those window boxes and finally had them nailed securely in place. Turning, my shoulder bumped a corner of the screen that covered the double-hung kitchen window. The screen dropped and hung precariously on two rusty nails. Let it hang for tonight; I'll fix it tomorrow, I thought, forgetting that the window had been opened wide to let in the fresh morning air.

Now it was past my usual dinnertime and I was exhausted. I had a quick bite to eat, then a long, leisurely shower. Looking in the mirror that shows no mercy, I saw the sags where once there were bumps, the long gray hair that curled over my shoulders, and the dismal realization that my body had betrayed me. Perhaps Charles was right—I've been too long in the country.

I could at least go to town and get my hair cut. But why? Why bother? I'm a seventy-five-year-old countrywoman. Who cares! Then, unbidden, came this thought: I wonder what Charles sees when he looks at me? Probably a fresh loaf of bread and an apple pie.

I pulled on an old flannel nightgown, the pink flowers long faded, with a collar buttoned at the throat. Warm and comfortable, nothing frivolous.

I appraised myself momentarily. At least I'm still size twelve but, for whatever reason, that thought dimmed.

Sitting in my old chair reading the evening paper with a cup of tea at my side, I was lured to bed by the thought of warm blankets and the content knowledge that the window boxes were up. I'd take care of the screen tomorrow.

Slipping into a deep, deep sleep, my subconscious betrayed me. I felt Charles's long fingers in my hair, felt the ribbons loosen, heard his voice whisper, "Red, you are my girl," and felt the joy of my first love.

A harsh scream wavered up and down and seemed to have no ending—it hung in the air like a plague, an unidentified sound that appeared to come from the kitchen. Terrified I looked at the illuminated dial of the clock—it read 3:15 AM. Trembling, I put my feet on the floor and crept down the dark hall. Near the kitchen, I pressed a switch and the room blazed with light. There—with its huge head completely filling the window, its mouth open, eyes blinking in the sudden light— stood an animal that looked almost prehistoric. Frantically I debated, shall I get Dad's gun and kill it? But then how would I ever get it out of the window? Its big dark eyes looked quietly at me. When it shook the gigantic head, I saw two banana-shaped ears that could only belong to a donkey.

My fear dissipated but left me weak and shaky…and then furious. Grabbing the broom with a shriek, I whacked it across the nose until it slowly withdrew its Jurassic Park head.

I slipped on my bedroom slippers and cursed my neighbor. Damn and double damn that Charles. This must be what he brought home in that trailer.

Not stopping to dress or even pull on a sweater, I ran out with the broom, flailed away at this huge gray animal and got it pointed in Charles's direction.

There was a full moon, and it was obvious that this was the biggest animal second only to elephants at the circus.

"Seventeen hands at least," Dad would have said.

I alternately swatted it with the broom and yelled, "Go! Go!" almost crying in despair as the donkey walked ever so slowly. It paid absolutely no attention to me or the broom.

The light in Charles's house came on. His voice called from the veranda, "Red, are you all right? Are you in trouble? Can I help you?"

"Damn right you can help. Come get your damn donkey before I shoot both of you."

He actually ran through the pasture. Breathless, he pleaded, "Oh, Red, I'm so sorry. Relax, take it easy. Don't be so upset. It's only an old donkey."

"Upset? Upset? It practically invaded my house. Scared me so badly I could have had a heart attack. Why did you bring this monstrosity here?"

"Well," he said, "I didn't exactly bring this donkey here, that was obviously her idea. I went to the auction today and they were going to sell her for dog meat. She looked at me as though she understood every word, so I just accidentally bought her for five dollars. She'll keep the grass down."

How could I compete with logic like that?

In the moonlight, a beautiful robe over his pajamas shined on this bank president from Tampa, Florida.

"Well, here she is now. Take her home and keep her there," I stormed.

She was waiting patiently, apparently waiting for us to finish.

"Red, how am I going to get her home?" he asked helplessly.

"Give her a swat with the broom and say 'giddyup'."

"Now you know I'm not going to do that."

"Damn it to hell!" With that, I reached over and yanked the sash from his robe, threw one end over her head, tied it together and handed him the fringed end.

I snarled, "Good night all," and turned to leave.

He stood petrified with astonishment.

The donkey turned with me and dragged Charles along. Picking up the broom, I yelled, "Now hang on and keep her moving. Go." She moved closer to me and lay that huge head on my shoulder. I could hear my bones crack.

Suddenly I was laughing. I said, "It's almost daylight. Here we are, me in my nightgown, your donkey wearing part of your clothing, and you in your pajamas. Who says dementia isn't among us? Hope the mailman doesn't come early—you've ruined my reputation."

I leaned momentarily against that mountain of gray.

"Let's give it one more try."

Ducking from under her head and walking quickly away, I felt her breath on my back.

"Charles, we're beaten. Give it up. I'll put her in my barn temporarily until you can work this out. Can you bring over some hay? Every rib in her body is plain to see."

"Best news I've heard in a long time. I don't know how to thank you, Red."

I walked and she followed as though that was what she had planned all along. I took her to my old barn and stayed with her, standing on tiptoe combing my fingers through what little mane she had, and murmuring soothing words to her.

Something inexpressible passed between us. Perhaps it was love.

That grizzled old head nuzzled close. As we stood together in the warm darkness, I felt her tremble against me as if she had run a long race and could hardly believe that she'd come in first.

I stroked her long ears and whispered, "We are both past our prime, but I promise you, we'll never go for dog meat."

CHAPTER 5

The rosy cloud in the east released the sun so Charles needed no light to bring in the hay. The only sound was the contented crunch of hay being consumed at a great rate.

With a heavy sigh, Charles said, "Red, I truly appreciate your help. I'll get that fellow who brought her and we'll get her out of here today."

Unbelievably, these words escaped from my own mouth: "Only if you want to be arrested for donkey stealing. They still hang people for that in Oregon. I'm keeping her, and I've named her 'DD' for 'damn donkey.'"

His eyes widened in surprise, but before he could utter a word, I said, "The sun is up so it must be breakfast time. I'll offer you fresh strawberry jam and hot cakes with syrup. Fair trade for this donkey."

"Shake on it," he said and took my hand. But when I tried to pull away, he held fast.

Just imagine two old people walking through the dew-covered grass, hand in hand. One in a well-worn nightgown that had lost its top button, the other striding along with his robe flapping with every step. Both literally covered with clinging hay and donkey hair.

Suddenly conscious of my ragged fingernails and rough, unkempt hands, I snatched my hand away. Walking ahead, I heard him say something to himself as he caught up to me. Somehow his voice sounded different.

"Red, you are the damndest woman I've ever known."

"Is that a compliment?" I demanded.

He hesitated. "Well, there was a girl in eighth grade…"

"Charles, look at us. We're a mess. Can we postpone this breakfast until tomorrow?"

"Of course," he answered, and left me at my door.

I heard my donkey and thought perhaps she was lonesome too. She met me at the barn door and hung her head over my shoulder. We stood warm and together in silent communication.

I thought about that donkey for hours. Because she was old, she probably had been passed from pillar to post. Judging from her long hooves and poor physical condition, she'd had little or no care, and was finally dumped at the auction for dog meat. I was so angry that sleep came slowly.

Nothing seemed to go right the next day. Broke one of my good dishes, dug up a whole row of carrot seeds just as they were beginning to sprout, burned a casserole. I looked at the window screen and thought, Why bother? This day is shot.

The next morning Charles was at the barn before I was.

"Red, surely we need to get a vet out here. She's so very thin."

"Yes, and a farrier too. Let's ask the woman at the feedstore—she'll know the best."

It must have been Charles's president-of-the-bank voice that brought both farrier and vet immediately. The donkey had few ailments other than starvation and long hooves, and all were taken care of at once. The farrier, whose name was Mickey McNeil, had short, curly hair as gray as mine. "We would have made a matched team," he said.

I felt complimented—although he was not movie-star handsome, he was surely not hard to look at. Not tall at five feet eight inches, but built like a tank with not an ounce of fat on him. Beneath a fine head of hair, his brown eyes always seemed to dance with a hidden joke.

"Do my own cookin'," he laughed. "Can't find anybody who wants to cook for a sixty-nine-year-old Irisher who likes a nip now and then."

I heard later that he was the most popular farrier in Oregon, but was now supposedly retired. Anyone who had a difficult horse called him. Mickey could sweet-talk any outlaw into complete submission, so said the lady at the feedstore.

Mickey chattered like a magpie as he examined the donkey's feet.

"Long, way too long," he said, shaking his head. "It will take quite a few trips to get those back in shape."

He stood with his hands on his hips and looked at her.

"That's just about the biggest donkey I've ever seen. Long ago, now I hardly remember, there was one about that size, maybe twenty years ago. She was a racer. Sure was something to see in that sulky. Famous all over the country. Then some guy from out of state paid a big price for her. Heard he was too handy with the whip so she quit on him. That was the last anybody heard of her. Where'd you get her?"

"At the auction," Charles answered.

"Yeah, figures. There's a rough old SOB that buys, sells and trades—goes to all the auctions, hauls 'em back, sells what he can and you know the rest."

I liked this little farrier. For starters, he spoke with an assurance that told me he knew his business, and he was gentle with my donkey. He talked donkey talk into one of those long ears before he lifted her foot. He said he had come from Ireland sixty years ago and added, "This thatch of gray hair had been black and curly then." At times he lapsed back into the heavy brogue of his homeland; seldom was there a lull in the conversation. He knew everyone for miles around— said he'd shod every horse in the country. He leaned over to lift one of her big feet.

"Very few of these mammoth donkeys are left. That's what she is, a mammoth. I imagine she was a fine specimen in her day. I'd guess she is at least thirty years old—not a tooth in her mouth. You'll need special feed," he added, setting her foot down after clipping and filing.

"That's all for today. I'll take more off that hoof next time. Don't want to lame her. She's sure no trouble to work on. What's her name?"

"Damned   Donkey,"   Charles   laughed.   "Red's corrupted me."

"Have not. I call her DD."

The barn where Charles's father had kept his fine Arabians had a tack room that contained everything for grooming. Charles brought over combs, brushes, anything he thought I could use, then leaned against the wall and watched.

"Red," he said, "I think I run a poor second to that donkey."

"Well," I answered, "you could come in first if your ears were longer."

She wandered the fence line whenever I was out, looking at me with those big, sad eyes. With my arms around her neck, her big head would nuzzle me as though she were counting every button.

When I couldn't sleep, the barn was my refuge. Her quiet nicker would tell me she was glad of my company. In the soft darkness, my feelings, some of which I'd never known before, poured out and her soft nudge would tell me that she understood with unconditional love.

My emotions were at war. My heart seemed to throb loudly enough to be heard and was accompanied by a warm flush that encompassed my entire body when I saw that tall man striding along the shortcut.

But in the next breath, I was so rude to him and wondered why he didn't take offense.

Why now? At this age? Ashamed at feeling like a silly schoolgirl with her first crush, I didn't even want to be his friend. If he is lonely, let him go to town. He'd find a lot of friends. A rich, good-looking bachelor—those ladies would get really friendly and he wouldn't be a bachelor very long.

I could go back to my peaceful life, my garden, my flowers, my donkey. Friends enough for me.

CHAPTER 6

Out in the garden one day, I looked up to see the mail carrier walking up Charles's driveway. I hurried to meet her. I had known the mail carrier was a woman, but had never had any reason to make her acquaintance.

"Hello," I said, extending my hand.

"Hello," she answered, brushing me off as she walked by.

Breathlessly trying to keep up with her long strides, I said, "Perhaps I can save you some time. I'm going right by Mr. Halstad's door and I can drop off his mail for you. It's quite a long walk and you seem to be in a hurry."

"Oh, no," she laughed, not slowing a step. "I think a man of Mr. Halstad's status should have personal service, don't you?" she added with a wicked little smile.

"I doubt it," I answered as I turned and walked over to my driveway, panting for breath.

Taking another look at this tall mail carrier, I was shocked to see so much of those long legs visible in shorts—shorts!— and all that red hair. Probably dyed.

I just happened to notice that it took her nearly forty minutes to deliver that letter, all the while standing on the veranda bold as brass.

The next day, while talking to Mickey while he worked, Charles joined us. I was so disgusted with him I could hardly say good morning.

During a lull in the conversation, Charles spoke.

"Mickey, do you happen to know the mail carrier?"

Mickey stood and rolled his eyes. "Tanzy Mullens—ain't she sumthin? Ever see a pair of hooters like those? Got to be a double D. All that artillery on one woman—and those legs. Wowee!"

Then, turning to me, he asked, "Whaddya think?"

He shouldn't have asked.

"I think the hooters are spectacular, especially if you like plastic, and the seismic reading must go through the ceiling as the cellulite quivers when she walks. Plus, she needs a haircut." This was the best I could do without sounding nasty.

"Now if you gentlemen will excuse me…"

Mickey's whoop of laughter and Charles's quiet chuckle escorted me out. For no reason, when I reached the house the door slammed behind me. Locating a pen and a sheet of writing paper, I scrawled a note.

"Miss Mullens, please hold my paper for sixty days as I will be out of town. Thank you, C. Halstad."

It was pretty authentic, I thought, as I slipped it into Charles's newspaper box.

A few days later Mickey was back. The donkey didn't look like the same animal. He's done wonders with her, and she surely stood square now. I looked up to see Charles saunter in with a "Hi" to Mickey and a nod to me.

"Charles! Tanzy, your mail carrier, told me you were gone for a couple of months," blurted Mickey in surprise.

The corners of Charles's mouth turned up in a grin, and I felt the flush that covered my face.

"That's odd," I lied. "My paper is there every night."

"I don't doubt it," Charles answered. "Perhaps I could come to your house and we could read it together tonight."

Caught in my own trap, I stuttered, "I'll give her a call. She's probably just confused."

As I left I heard Mickey's voice and something about "jealous." Well, they weren't talking about me—I don't have a jealous bone in my body. And then, "Would take a big man to put a halter on that one."

"I know just the man if he could find the halter," Charles said.

What is it with men? The halter hung on the same peg it always has.

The Irishman's sense of humor kept us amused, and I enjoyed bantering with the feisty little guy and listening to his outrageous opinions of various neighbors. It was always pie and coffee when he was done working.

One day, after Mickey had gone, Charles lingered over his third cup of coffee. I got nervous. Finally, he said, "You know, Red, you get along so well with Mickey, I'm almost jealous."

Turning from the cupboard, I asked "Jealous of what? He may be a better farrier, but I doubt he could chair a committee as well."

He stood and, as I turned, placed a hand on either side of me. I was trapped.

"Red, I've had many opportunities in the past, but I've always waited for the right one."

I closed my eyes, afraid of what he was going to say—or not say.

A quick knock at the door and Mickey's voice interrupted, " 'Scuse me, I've forgotten my clippers. Did you notice where I put them?"

The spell was broken.

CHAPTER 7

"I think I'll take a drive over to the auction. Sure would be nice to have a good milk cow—my own butter and cream—and she could help keep the grass down."

"Charles, who in the world is going to milk this cow?"

"Oh, I'm sure one of the local lads would like to earn a few dollars."

I smirked. "All of the local lads would enlist in the Iranian army before they'd pull a tit."

He looked pained. "I thought those things were called 'teats.'"

"Well, Oregon tits are different from Florida teats."

"Really? I thought all cows were the same," he said in honest astonishment.

"Do you mind if I go with you? Perhaps be of some help," I offered, hoping to distract him from this latest bit of folly.

"Be delighted to have you. I am a little vague about cows, although the *Farmers' Almanac* has been a great help."

My first glimpse of the house of horrors made me nauseous. The noise, the stench, the pitiful animals that were rushing around in the ring, the ringmaster cracking a big whip, the auctioneer lying through his teeth about the wonderful quality of the animals there. In my opinion, they were the rejects of the animal world.

"Oh, look at that fine specimen," Charles exclaimed as a young spotted bull rushed past. Charles held up his numbered card, waving it wildly.

I jerked the card from his hand. "Charles! Surely a bank president can distinguish between a bull and a cow. That big pink thing wasn't an udder!"

"Well," he answered, "She ran by so fast I couldn't tell if she had a disease. We may as well go home."

As we made our way through the crowd, something in the ring caught my eye. A small gray donkey. Must be a dwarf, I thought. So thin, so frightened running around the ring, the big whip cracking at her heels. The auctioneer bawled harshly: "A real purebred miniature donkey only thirty inches at the shoulder, all the way from Missouri. What am I bid?"

I held the card up high, then higher, and she was mine for fifteen dollars. My mind blurred. What have I done? Not usually given to impulses, I was certain that a sudden illness had overtaken me.

Charles looked at me strangely.

Embarrassed, I held my card up high again and yelled, "Run her through again. No sale! No sale!"

A sharp crack of the whip and here she came again, eyes rolling in fear, running in circles, the man with the whip never far behind.

Now I could see the dark patches of sweat on her heaving sides. Finally she stood panting for breath, trembling, then raised her head to look directly into my eyes. Some unknown force lifted my hand and she was mine for twenty-five dollars.

Furious at myself, I held back the angry tears—to think I had raised my own bid and bought a donkey as useful to me as a camel.

Charles found someone to deliver the poor little thing and she led willingly to his barn. He was thrilled.

"Look, look! She lets me lead her."

"Charles, when is your birthday?"

"In the fall."

"Well, happy birthday to you and give your present a drink of water. You can have some of DD's hay."

He looked at me, astounded. "No one has ever given me a gift that pleased me more. Thank you, thank you, Red. Let me take you home. You look tired, Emma."

"Thank you, but I need the exercise."

That was the first time he'd called me Emma.

Almost dancing down the well-worn path with my heart racing, my breath catching in short gasps, I thought, I don't remember that exercise has ever made me feel this way before.

The next morning Charles came down the shortcut— now a well-beaten path—with the docile little donkey leading beside him carrying her big belly on four spindly legs.

"The vet can't come until tomorrow unless it's an emergency. It isn't, is it?" he asked anxiously. "Could she be pregnant?"

"Of course not, probably just starved and wormy. The vet will take care of that tomorrow and in a few weeks you won't recognize her. Don't worry. What did you name her?"

"Birthday Girl," he smiled and added, "Mickey is bringing over a book he found about donkeys. I'll need to learn something about them."

"Hope he remembers his damned tools this time," he muttered. But I heard him, turned my head so he didn't see the laughter that was choking me. Yet in my secret heart, I, too, wished Mickey's memory hadn't failed him.

It was "Emma" yesterday, but tonight it was "Red, Red," with a hard knock on the door.

"Oh, Charles, for goodness sakes. What is it that can't wait until morning? It's eleven o'clock."

"Oh, Red, she's sick, really sick. She's rolling all around, trying to get up and I think I see blood. Please come."

I pulled on my jeans and an old sweater and together we almost ran to the barn, the lantern swinging between us.

"I've been worried, and the last time I checked her, she wouldn't get up."

It didn't take my nursing certificate to see that she was definitely trying to deliver a foal—the hard way. Only one foot and a wet floppy ear showed with each contraction. She strained and rolled. Nothing more appeared.

"Charles, I've got to straighten that baby or they are both going to die."

"What can I do, Red? How can I help?"

"Hold the lantern steady."

I rolled up my sleeve as far as it would go and washed my arm and hand in a fresh pail of water that Charles had brought for her. On my knees, my hand followed the little ear back to its destination. I found the head and turned it with every contraction, working together with Birthday Girl, but her efforts were slowing and I knew that time was running out.

"One more time, girl, one more. Hold the lantern closer, Charles."

Finally, I found the other leg and straightened it as, with one massive grunt, she pushed out two tiny front hooves with the nose resting on top—in its proper position—then a shoulder, one more push, and a very wet baby slid out and lay there for a moment without moving, gasping for breath.

Looking at Charles, I saw on his face a look of wonderment. I noticed it was wet with sweat too.

"Hey, I did all the work. Why are you sweating?"

"Red, I've never seen anything born before. It is a miracle—a live baby nurtured for how many months from its mother's blood."

"Charles, I think we can safely say this baby was preconceived—have to give the sire some credit. Different from chickens."

As I washed in the cold water, he pulled out the always-spotless handkerchief to dry on. Returning it, he caught my hand and kissed it.

"Thank you, thank you, Red, for the many things you've taught me and the special friendship you've given me. You've made my life almost complete."

I didn't know how to respond to such a tribute, so I said nothing. In the dark of the lantern, my tears begged for release. No other man had ever found me so worthy.

"Red, you must be exhausted. It's almost two o'clock."

"Yes, I am."

So saying, I sat down on a pile of sweet-smelling hay. He stood for a moment as if undecided, then hung the lantern on a peg and sat down beside me. Together we watched the baby stumble to its feet, fall, then stand up again, trembling on its shaky legs. The tired little mother stood cleaning her baby as it nursed.

I leaned back and closed my eyes.

It was the first light of day when I awoke to find Charles's arm around my shoulder and his jacket covering me. He was still asleep in his shirtsleeves. At my movement, he awoke and sat up quickly with a big smile.

"Good morning, Red. Best sleep I ever had."

Wordless, I handed him his jacket.

"Now that I've compromised you, I think we should get married," he laughed. "Will you? Will you marry me, Red?"

Then he turned and was all lopsided trying to balance on one knee.

My heart was beating so, I could hardly breathe. My old bones struggled in the hay to regain my footing, and I fled down the path to my own kitchen with my mind in turmoil.

What if Mickey had come early? We would have been the scandal of the neighborhood.

I showered, combed the hay out of my hair, and dressed. After several cups of very black coffee, I headed to the barn to feed DD. Mickey was already there.

"Oh, Red, you're early. Or I am. This girl is done for the present. Four beautiful hooves if I do say so myself, and she looks like a million bucks too."

"Hear that, DD?" I pulled down one of her long ears to whisper the good news when I noticed there were some strange little marks, almost looked like letters.

"Mickey, look at this. These dark blue marks."

He pulled her big head down as I held the ear open, squinting as he spit on his sleeve and rubbed the dust away.

"I'll be damned," he said. "I read 'ESM1945-1.' You got a pencil?"

"Pencil? What are you two up to?" Charles interrupted.

"Quick, quick, write this down," Mickey demanded, repeating "ESM1945-1."

Mickey was almost jumping up and down with excitement.

"This donkey is the famous Esmeralda. The donkey that won everything from a quarter-mile race to halter classes all over the state."

I hadn't dared to look at Charles yet.

"Can you really be sure?" I asked.

"Yep, there are the tattoos. If we had the cart and harness, I could show you in a minute. I'll bet that old scoundrel at the auction yard has the cart out in the junkyard— couldn't sell it. Too big for anything else. Probably get it for a song."

I was so excited at the thought that I could hardly contain myself.

"Yes, yes! I'll get some money. How much do you need?"

Charles stepped forward with a roll of bills. "Take what you need."

Mickey was off in a flash, his old pickup leaving a trail of exhaust. I puttered around, not looking or speaking to Charles.

Esmeralda stood between us. I told her, "No more 'DD'—now it will be Ezzy for short."

I picked up a brush. Smiling, Charles stepped around the donkey and said, "Me first. Get the hay out of my hair or Mickey might suspect. It's not every night I sleep in the barn, but if you're willing…"

"Charles, damn you. Don't you dare make fun of me." I raised the brush, and quick as a cat he came forward and pinned my arms to my side. He held me so tight I couldn't even kick him.

"Red, Red, stop. What will it take to prove to you that I love you and want to be with you the rest of my life?"

The question was warm on his lips when suddenly the door flung open and Mickey's voice, loud and exuberant, intruded.

"I got the works for a song, Faith and Begorrah, I did! Ten dollars delivery," he sang as he danced a little jig. He tossed the roll of bills to Charles, who promptly threw it back and growled, "Keep it and take a month's vacation."

Mickey laughed, clapped a hand to his leg, and said, "I knew you'd find the halter!"

I couldn't take any more excitement. I found a pan and went to the garden to shell peas, try to compose myself, and figure out where my life was going.

After a long, serious talk with myself, the peas went flying in every direction.

I need to let my thoughts reason through this tangle of emotions that clogged my brain. "Be logical and honest, Emma," surprised to hear those words spoken out loud.

Do you really believe he loves you? Love is for young people. Could it be that he is just lonely? Well, he didn't take much interest in Tanzy, and he's been single in Florida for many years, and there are plenty of opportunities in town for a lonely, rich bachelor. No, I don't think he's lonely. Is he just playing? I'm something different—just a novelty. What about my wrinkles? My hands don't look like the Florida girls. I only use soap and water on my skin. No wonder I'm wrinkled.

But he is awfully good to me. Always courteous, even when I'm obnoxious.

But my mind protested. I'm just not in his class. How would he feel about introducing me to his friends in Florida as Mrs. Charles Halstad? But surely he would have thought about that before he asked. My psyche played the devil's advocate.

Emma, do you love him? Probably. I don't know, really, what love is. I read once where love was the intense desire to please. Well, he qualifies for that, but I don't go out of my way to please him. Oh, no? What about doubling your baking days when you should be in the garden? What about babysitting his donkey, and helping him cut the barbwire from his tractor wheels after he ran the fence down. You are just too old-maidish to take a chance. Coward.

If it isn't love, why do you feel so wonderful when he's around? Why do you watch for him to come down the shortcut? Shame on you, you coward.

I just need a little more time to be certain. Sure you do. You're almost seventy-six and he's almost eighty. You've got lots of time, coward.

That does it. I tossed the last of the peas to the birds and walked up to the big barn where Charles and the vet were admiring the baby. The vet had disinfected the little donkey's navel and medicated the mother.

An adorable, fuzzy little animal came just to Charles's knee. We watched her play, completely unafraid of her new world. She nursed loudly and often as her mother munched hay contentedly.

"Red, did you ever see anything so adorable?"

When she looked at me with those big, dark eyes, what could I say?

I had never seen a man so happy about an animal, not even Mr. Halstad with his expensive Arabians. To him, they were just livestock. It was easy to see that these donkeys were family to Charles. But who was I to talk? What was Ezzy to me?

As we walked back to the house, Charles was beaming. I had to hurry to keep up with his long strides.

"What shall I name her? Her mother is Birthday Girl, so I guess I'll just call her 'Baby Girl.' What do you think?"

"I don't think I've ever seen a person so delighted with so little. I'm happy for you that everything turned out so well. It was a miracle."

"We slept pretty well too," Charles gave me a sly look. "Wonder what the younger generation would have thought if they had seen us—two senior citizens all cuddled up in the hay?"

"I was not all cuddled up," was my indignant reply.

"Well, I was," Charles laughed. "And if you weren't, I certainly was fooled."

"Couldn't have been much of a cuddle if I slept through it," came my sarcastic response.

He stopped in the middle of the path, in broad daylight, and pulled me to him, holding me so tightly that I could hardly breathe. When I dared to open my eyes and look up, his flushed face told me my nasty barb had found its mark.

"Perhaps I can do better in the daylight."

His unexpected reach held my struggling body and, tilting my chin with a finger, he proceeded to slowly and thoroughly kiss every part of my face. Feelings I had never known existed stormed to the surface. His hands now were linked behind me and I melted into his lean, lanky body. My breath came hard and fast, my arms reached upward without any help from me, and all I wanted was that this moment last forever.

Releasing me, he stepped away.

"Emma, obviously you didn't sleep through that. I won't bother you again. Now, if you'll excuse me…," he said, walking away.

Standing for a moment, my shaking knees hardly supported me. I could still feel his warm mouth on my face, feel his hands, his body pressed close. All my senses were alive and screaming.

With my mind still whirling, I slowly walked the path and collapsed in a chair, closed my eyes, and relived the entire episode, trying to push back the sounds of his last words: "I won't bother you again."

CHAPTER 8

Eight days and sleepless nights without a word. Doubt and anger confused my mind. Was my thoughtless remark going to permanently erase the love he had declared for me? Or was it just his opportunity to make a graceful exit?

My first fears were justified. I had known from the beginning that it was only a pipe dream—too wonderful to be real.

Get over it, Emma, I sniffled. Act your age.

Days were always busy, but I never knew that nights could stretch into months. Many hours of these nights were spent in the barn with Ezzy and, after my "donkey therapy," I felt better. I realized that she didn't know why I was unhappy, but without doubt she sensed something was not right with me. Leaning against that mountain of comfort, my woes seemed to melt. Her unconditional love was her wordless offering.

The sweet, clean smell of hay, the splash of moonlight that lingered in the doorway, the faraway song of the crickets.

Taking it all in, I sat on a bale of hay trying to evade the memories that besieged me.

The feeling of his arms about me and the prayer that he would "bother" me until the end of my days never left me. Happiness had been at my door, but I had been too stubborn and scared to answer the doorbell.

I made an extra-large pie to present to Charles with my heartfelt apologies, and hurried because I could see Charles at my barn with Mickey, who was holding a measuring stick against Ezzy's shoulder. Apparently Mickey had somehow finagled her old cart and harness. I hurriedly took my apron off, but too late. I heard the sound of Charles's car as he drove away with Mickey beside him.

My girl was in the pasture rolling away in the deep grass any inconvenience she may have had with the measuring stick.

Two days later, the sulky and harness were delivered. I walked to the barn to find Mickey and Charles in deep conversation. He nodded a cool "Good morning" to me and walked away.

Mickey was almost in tears. The harness was ruined because of its exposure to the elements.

"Ah, tis a shame, a fine leather, it was."

He laughed when he told me of the deliveryman's quick exit when the remnants of the sulky were unloaded.

The incredibly large wheels—one, no longer circular; the other, worse. Two shaves, one splintered beyond use.

Mickey cursed at the waste and stormed off, the exhaust from his old pickup marking his passage.

I was disappointed too. In my imagination, Ezzy and I, in all her glory, would drive about the property just for fun.

Hardly had my coffee cooled enough for my first sip when there was a quick rap at the door. For a moment I hoped… but it was Mickey who bounced in.

"You're pretty spry this morning," I laughed. "Shouldn't you conserve your strength at your age?"

He ignored that remark.

With his eyes sparkling, he nearly danced. "Faith and Begorrah, I have searched my memory to remember where that shop was that built and repaired wagons and carts, and, like a revelation from Saint Peter himself, it came to me in the middle of the night. It is in a little town, Klamath Falls, about forty miles from here. I must tell Charles."

Grateful for their help and interest, I still felt excluded from this exciting development. It didn't seem as though I was part of anything anymore.

Watching from my kitchen window, I saw Charles and Mickey take careful measurements. They were laughing like two schoolboys, then they were off.

My day was spent repainting the flower boxes and reinforcing the rose trellis, which was by now a blaze of color.

Tomorrow, the window screen. I promise.

Bright rays of the sun crept over my face. With a start, I realized I'd overslept—understandable since sleep had been intermittent. But guilt got the better of me despite the fact that my garden was weedless, my house tidy.

Dressed, I made a pot of coffee and took it to the porch where I sat on the top step enjoying both the strong black brew and the view of Mount Grayback, snowcapped still, but dark with the trees that covered it. Ezzy nickered. She's telling me that breakfast is late, I thought. Hurrying to the barn, I found that she had been fed and had fresh water. Not a sign of Mickey. Surely not Charles.

She followed me and we walked. She stopped occasionally for a quick roll in the spring grass or just to put her head over my shoulder as I scratched behind those long ears and whispered things I never would have revealed to anyone else.

The hours passed. I knew that window screen was waiting, but it could wait longer. Still, this was the day. I convinced myself that when the sun was at my back would be the best time.

Sure enough, at last the sun was there.

I rounded the house to find the screen still where it had fallen. Following Mickey's line of reasoning, I had dared to hope that perhaps the fairies had carried it away.

I had mislaid my hammer. In my mind, I could see it sitting on top of my old ladder. While searching, I became impatient and decided to use Dad's big heavy hammer instead.

I found long nails and an old kitchen chair that wasn't too steady. But for goodness sakes, that screen needed only four nails—a ladder really wasn't essential. Just a few whacks with that hammer and that little chore that had nagged me would be done. I laughed remembering how Ezzy had stuck her head in that window.

After placing the chair under the window, the stretch seemed a few inches higher than I'd thought. I momentarily wished for the ladder. I managed to stand unsteadily on the rickety surface, finally positioning the screen, and pulled Dad's hammer from under my belt. With a whack, the first corner was secure. The chair wobbled, but there were only three more nails to go. Quickly, two more were in. Breathing a sigh of relief, I reproached myself for having put off such a simple job for so long.

Upon tapping the fourth and final nail just hard enough to secure it, I triumphantly slammed the heavy hammer in the general direction of the nail as the chair splintered beneath me. Unerringly the hammer made a crushing connection with my thumb.

I screamed and fell to my knees in the dirt, then rolled into a fetal position amid the remnants of the chair. Crying hysterically, bloody, and dirty, I struggled to get up.

Then I felt his arms as he lifted me. A white handkerchief wiped my face, then wrapped around my bloody hand.

"C'mon, Red, let's get that cleaned up and on ice."

Leaning heavily against him, he led me to his car in my driveway that in a moment was parked in his.

Arms around me, he almost carried me into the house. I held my throbbing hand and the rest of my body screamed in sympathy.

He guided me to a bathroom where we managed to remove my dirty shirt. I stood in my bra, shaking, uncaring, as he gently unwound the handkerchief that would never be white again. Tenderly, he washed my hand until the water ran clear. I put my arms into a shirt that he held, and from nowhere a hand brushed the hair that had fallen across my face.

"Red, sit down for a moment and let me put some ice on that."

He seated me on a large brocaded sofa and placed an ice bag on a pillow, resting my hand on it.

"Does that help?"

"Not much," I groaned.

"Would you like something cool to drink?" he asked.

"Oh, yes, my throat is raw."

He brought me a cool drink of something I couldn't identify, but it was wonderful. Wordlessly, I held out my glass for another, then one more.

"Why don't you relax for a minute. When it feels better, I'll take you home," Charles suggested.

When I awoke, it was to find the pillow under my head and a blanket covering my bare feet. For a moment I couldn't place my surroundings. Then realization struck.

I struggled to a sitting position, my head whirling. My bandaged thumb was throbbing as I tried to stand, making it on the third try. The ice bag fell and landed between my shoes.

My gaze focused on a man sitting by the window reading. He looked up and laid his book down. "Feeling better now?"

"What time is it?"

He stood and looked at his watch. "Almost six."

"You mean I've been asleep most of the night? Here? What was in that drink?"

He looked guilty. "Oh, Red, really nothing much. Orange juice and perhaps just a little medicinal vodka."

"Vodka? You've plied me with liquor, half undressed me. What else have you done?"

"Not what I would have done forty years ago," he laughed.

Furious, I flung my shoe at him. He caught it in midair.

"Guess I didn't tell you that I was the catcher for the Tampa Tigers for nine years. Now, how are you going to walk with one shoe?"

"I'll walk barefoot if I have to," I replied, limping to the door with one shoe.

Following me out, he knelt and tied both shoes as I sat fuming on the veranda steps. Starting down the path, I heard his steps behind me. I was at the door when his voice sounded, "Good morning then, Red. Try to keep ice on that."

I turned. "You haven't spoken to me for eight days and now I'm sorry I've bothered you. And I'm sincerely sorry I was so rude eight days ago."

He looked at his watch. "Eight days, six hours and thirty-eight minutes by my time."

"Now you are bothering me, Mr. Halstad."

He grinned, "According to plan, Emma."

My heart gave a giant leap of joy, but I closed the door firmly. Two can play at that game. He won't see me for a lot longer than eight days.

I did keep ice on that steadily throbbing thumb, but to no avail. I walked the floor carrying it in my other hand. Finally, I removed the bandages to see a horribly discolored and swollen thumb. My experienced eye told me that it was probably broken at the first joint. I made a makeshift splint and rebandaged it. The pain intensified as the evening approached with not even an aspirin in the house. Desperate, I decided to bother Mr. Halstad for some of that medicinal orange juice or suffer all night.

He must have seen me coming up the path because the veranda lights came on and the door opened before I could knock.

"Emma! What a delightful surprise. Come in and have a cup of tea. How is the thumb?"

"Miserable. The ice packs don't help. I was hoping for something other than tea. Perhaps a small glass of that medicinal orange juice."

Two highball glasses and a pitcher appeared as if by magic.

"To us," he toasted, and to us, I drank.

After the first sip, I observed, "Is this the same medicine you gave me last night? Doesn't seem quite the same."

"That's easily remedied."

My next glass told me he was a little easier on the orange juice.

The pain seemed to subside a little and I relaxed.

"Charles, whatever brought you back to this deserted farm in Oregon?"

"Forty years in the banking business was all I'd ever done, and that was all work. Not much time for anything else. I had a few good friends, but I was always the fifth wheel that they were trying to marry off. After all those years in the business world, I thought I'd better see if there was anything else in the universe. About the only thing that came to mind was this farm. But I tried a beautiful retirement home first, and it was everything they said it would be, but it was full of old people and I was bored to death. It was 'dearie this' and 'dearie that,' bingo on Tuesdays, tea and cookies, amorous ladies with fancy, colored hair, and food out of a can with a cherry on top. I knew there had to be something more and I had to find it before I got too old.

"I had many memories of the old schoolhouse, the farm and of you, but, of course, I'd thought that you'd married and moved on. When I asked the contractor about the adjoining farm, he told me that a gray-haired lady lived there alone very independently. That's why he got a bonus for a rush job.

"I just packed some clothes, canceled my lease, called for my car and drove almost nonstop. Best decision I ever made. I found the same Emma I loved in eighth grade—you haven't changed a bit."

My defenses trembled like the Walls of Jericho, and suddenly the years dropped away and I wasn't seventy-five anymore.

"Charles, I've never said that I love you."

"Oh, yes, you have. Eight days ago on the path, your response told me what I believed to be true. But say it now. I'll never hear it enough."

He moved to sit beside me on the sofa.

"I love you, Charles."

With my good arm I brought his head down and kissed him as he had kissed me on the path. I had never felt so safe, so loved, so sure.

"We must get married at once…"

His murmuring voice planned far into the night. I fell asleep in his arms.

Together like two spoons, we awoke in the morning.

I think I mentioned it was a large sofa.

CHAPTER 9

Rousing from a deep sleep, I tried to turn but there seemed to be an obstruction. Then came a warm kiss in the vicinity of my ear and his whisper, "May we always awaken like this."

At last, all my defenses were down and I was comfortable in his love.

Turning my head, the sight of a nearby nightstand brought most of the previous evening to mind—two long-stemmed glasses, a half-full vodka bottle, a pitcher of orange juice—and I suddenly realized my thumb had recovered.

Charles departed for the kitchen to make coffee, and I to the bathroom, hoping to find a brush to tame my wild hair.

Charles had finally learned to make a decent cup of coffee, and, as we sat at the table, we planned.

"Let's go to Portland and get a marriage license. We could be married by this time next week," Charles enthused.

I protested with women's age-old cry, "I haven't a thing to wear."

"We'll shop! You'll have the finest of everything—wedding dress, ring—your heart's desire. I'll call Mickey—he'll take care of the animals."

So in my dowdy clothes, we went to Portland four days later, and when I came home, "dowdy" was only a word in the dictionary.

Portland was in a different world. I awoke in a bed big enough to accommodate an entire family, but it appeared as though only one side had been used, and I was in it. I looked about at the luxurious surroundings. The suite of rooms was larger than my entire house.

Charles stood in the doorway, precariously balancing a tray laden with a coffeepot, cups, and fancy pastries. "Room service," he laughed, as he carefully deposited it on a table.

I tried to get up, but he gently pushed me back.

"Haven't you ever had breakfast in bed?" he asked.

"Charles, I look a fright, let me up."

He sat on the edge of the bed, looking down.

"Red, you are a beautiful woman. Not the beauty that comes from a box, but the deep inner beauty that never fades."

Then, in my heart, I wasn't a wrinkled, opinionated seventy-five-year-old farm woman. I was a beautiful princess, young and alive, and in love. My arms reached up and pulled his unprotesting body down, then reached for the covering.

Later, he said, "I was mistaken about this hotel—it was declared to be the best in Portland, but now look. The coffee is cold and the pastries are stale."

The next few days were a whirlwind of activity. The first thing we did was apply for our marriage license.

I laughed—we'd had the honeymoon before the wedding.

Charles rented a limousine with a driver and we toured the city. I saw a Portland I had never known existed—museums, art galleries, beautiful shops. And overlooking the serene river were restaurants that promised food that would have sent any world traveler into ecstasy. I couldn't even read the menu.

"I need to make known that my intentions are honorable," Charles declared. He tapped the window that separated us from the cab driver.

"Find us the best jewelry store in town."

Upon arrival, the jeweler presented trays of so many blazingly beautiful rings, I was too spellbound to choose. So Charles chose and, of course, it was the one my eyes had lingered on.

"I do not need two rings," I protested.

"Of course you do. Don't you want a wedding ring?" Charles asked.

My mind whirled and I felt my knees shake as the man fitted the rings to my finger. Charles was delighted and said slyly, "See what that night in the haymow has brought about?"

I wanted to say something, but the look on the young jeweler's face restrained me. Charles kissed my hand as he placed a beautiful solitaire on my finger.

"Not another step until we stop for a cup of tea. I'm exhausted by your extravagances."

Charles laughed. "I was going to buy you the Hope Diamond, but they didn't have it in stock. Now for a wedding dress."

Following his accustomed way of life, he instructed the driver to take us to the finest dress shop in the city. In my modest blouse, plain skirt, and shoes not much better than my barn boots, I would rather be anywhere, anywhere, than in the doorway of this fancy establishment.

But I wanted to be all I could be for Charles. Holding that thought, I stepped bravely over the threshold into the clutches of an eager saleslady.

Charles informed her that we wanted a very special dress for a very special occasion—our wedding. She assured us that we had come to the right place.

"What color, Emma?"

"Blue," I answered.

Charles made himself comfortable, stretching his legs in front of a big chair. The saleslady, obviously younger than me by about twenty years, led me to the dressing room.

"Just hang your clothes there and I'll be back in a moment. I want to see what we have in blue that you might like."

Only my mirror had ever seen me naked. I staved off panic when I reminded myself that we women all have the same equipment. I hung my skirt and blouse and kicked off my shoes and panties. She reappeared, drew the curtain and turned to see me standing naked except for a bra.

"Oh, miss, miss, you don't have a foundation garment?" Shock registered on her face.

Well, to me, a bra was a foundation garment, but somehow the bra was riding high above its cargo.

"Oh, my…," I flushed with embarrassment. "They've gone south."

The twinkle in her eye and the smile she tried to disguise suddenly irritated me.

"Don't laugh at me. You aren't just out of the nest yourself, missy. It won't be too long before mine will be singing 'Hello Dolly' to those in your fancy bra."

At that, we both broke into giggles like two schoolgirls. As she wiped her eyes, she said, "I guess I'll just take you under my wing. We'll start from the bottom up. There's a great shoe store just around the corner. You'll need heels, two inches at least. Then, of course, undergarments." Then she brought me a bra "just like hers," she remarked. We laughed and suddenly my youth was restored—almost.

"The rest of you doesn't need any help," she added. "Hope I look that good at seventy-five."

We chatted like old friends. She laughed again. "We needn't hurry, the bridegroom is asleep in his chair and it's almost closing time."

We were having fun. I tried on everything from stockings to lingerie—I never knew satin could feel so good.

She brought in four gorgeous blue gowns. No way could they be called dresses. I chose a soft, misty-blue chiffon that fit perfectly. The new bra added interest to the low neckline. I stepped out to nudge a dozing Charles.

His first words were, "That's it. Emma, you couldn't have chosen better."

My self-confidence bloomed under his admiring gaze.

"Pack up everything she needs and wants and send them to this address." Charles handed her the hotel's card.

"Your lady needs some time at the spa," she suggested. "We've had a wonderful time, but I know she's tired."

We hugged good-bye, and I was whisked away to an establishment I had only read about, where I was massaged with sweet-smelling oil, manicured, pedicured, and treated to my first facial. My hair was piled high—I didn't like it, but Charles did. This isn't the "Red" of years past, but what was so great about being Red? Broken fingernails, aching back, sunburn. This is my new life about to begin. My heart seemed to be beating in double time. Looking up at this handsome man beside me, his long fingers curled around mine, I knew this was the right time for us.

Those blue eyes that were looking down at this stylishly dressed woman with the curly gray hair, now professionally coiffed, saw the woman in baggy jeans and work-torn shirt and loved them both the same.

Clinging to his arm as we left the spa, I asked, "Well, what do you think?"

"I think I am the luckiest man in the world."

Tears ran down my cheeks, ruining my mascara and leaving dark smudges on his immaculate handkerchief.

"While you were at the spa, our driver told me of a little stone church he had been baptized in years ago. I had to see it, so he drove me out there. It's on the outskirts of a small, rural town. An old church with a belfry like something out of a storybook. You'll love it."

Stopping momentarily to catch his breath, he added, "Tomorrow at five, that bell will ring for Mr. and Mrs. Halstad. The minister told me that the church was eighty years old and that his wife would play the organ."

His joyous voice went on and on, but his eyes blurred as he said, "We've saved the best for last."

That night sleep came fitfully.

Occasionally in years past, I would awaken to feel deep in my being the loneliness and an unexplainable yearning. But with the morning, my rational mind would assure me it was just a passing thought and I really shouldn't eat dinner so late.

Now when I awake, I have no need to stare at the ceiling. Feeling the loving warmth of outstretched arms, hearing the gentle snore that made me know this man was real, I would find him beside me when the sun had chased the dark away.

This was our wedding day. The morning dawned bright and clear. Charles was already up polishing his already spotless shoes. I tied the sash about my soft satin robe and tried to ignore the strange feeling in my stomach.

With a knock at the door, a fabulous breakfast was wheeled in and Charles poured coffee with a flourish and a happy, "Good morning." He ate heartily as I sat beside him, but I couldn't swallow a bite.

"Surely you're not nervous," he grinned.

"Of course I'm not nervous," came my testy reply as my coffee cup slipped from my shaking fingers. "Let's go home," I blurted.

Ignoring the coffee that trickled freely, he looked at me in surprise, then pulled me down to his lap and kissed my tears.

"Don't tease me, Red. Those are tears of happiness, right?"

"Right," I said, burrowing my head in his shoulder, my tears dripping like a leaky faucet.

His voice was comforting as he held me and talked about the places we could go—wonderful things we could do, our happy life together. Then he was quiet. I could sense his bewilderment and shock, and shame crept over me and my conscience berated me for what I was—a coward. Shame for the hurt I had given him.

"Excuse me a moment," I said, pulling away.

Retreating to the bedroom, I dropped my robe, then quickly lifted my beautiful blue dress from its padded hanger and slipped it over my head. Sliding my feet into the two-inch heels, I walked out smiling and wiping my nose.

Charles was at the window, looking but not seeing.

"Charles," my voice trembled. "Look."

He turned to see me. As I walked into his arms held wide, I knew I was home.

Later, it took me two hours to dress. I worried. Is this dress a little short? What if I stumbled in these new high-heeled shoes? Surely that didn't dare to be a hangnail. Charles was elegant in a dark suit, a smile and a twinkle in his eye.

We were early. I had wanted to see this church that had so enthralled Charles. The driver said it truly was eighty years old; the dates were chiseled in stone.

Centered in a sea of soft waving grass suggested that church services had not been regular. Built in the country, the little village had grown around it.

I was awed by my first impression of this little stone church still standing proud after all these years. A faint sound from above told me the bell still occupied the belfry.

A blooming hedge was a charming backdrop concealing a parking lot with only a limousine and a bored driver as today's occupants.

My amazement at this little old stone structure grew steadily as I stared at the unpretentious beauty of the stones as they hugged together, outlining the deep-set lead-glass windows and arched doorway.

The dusty gray of the stones was softened by the soft yellow of tenacious honeysuckle that clung to every possible surface—forgiven perhaps because of the fragrance that drifted in the air like a benediction.

It was the music from a magnificent old organ, music that I would never forget, that summoned us.

We held hands as we walked slowly down the aisle to the smiling pastor. Charles, elegant in his dark suit, me walking tall in my high heels, my beautiful chiffon dress flowing gracefully with every step.

First a prayer, then we repeated after the pastor the sacred vows.

"Do you, Charles Halstad, take Emma Lindstrom as your lawfully wedded wife, to love and to cherish through sickness and health for as long as you both shall live?"

Tears stood in Charles's eyes as he answered, "I do."

I repeated the vows in a voice firm and sure.

As Charles slipped the ring on my finger, the pastor said, "I now pronounce you man and wife," and with a broad smile, he added, "You may now kiss the bride." Charles showed no reluctance and I returned his kiss with conviction.

As we walked out the door, the bell in the belfry sounded loud and clear. The pastor was surprised.

"It must have been a gust of wind. I can't remember the last time it rang."

With the pastor's blessing, "May you always walk together," we collected our driver. I looked back at the little church and wished it another eighty years.

Charles turned to me. "It took a lot of effort to get you to the altar, and I've worked up an appetite. I think a celebration is appropriate."

He spoke to the driver. "If you had just married the girl of your dreams, in what extraordinary restaurant would you celebrate your first meal as man and wife?"

"Martinez, the best on the river. Very exclusive, wonderful food. Quiet, music, even a small dance floor. Oh, and a fine bar."

I seated myself carefully, not wanting to wrinkle my dress, and slipped off my fancy heels. The left one pinched.

"We'll take a cab later," Charles said, and put something in the man's hand that brought a big smile.

I quickly replaced my shoes.

The restaurant was everything our driver had described. We ate a leisurely dinner, which was outstanding and impeccably served. A bottle of wine, in a bucket of ice at Charles's elbow, was poured generously by the waiter, who declared it to be the best in the state.

I liked it much better than vodka and orange juice and lifted my glass again. Charles sipped.

I excused myself to go to the powder room. Upon my return, Charles said with a grin, "You surely are a fine figure of a woman—even without your shoes."

Embarrassed, my feet fumbled under the table until I was relieved to have those heels pinching my toes again.

I held up my glass that had been quietly refilled, stood a bit unsteadily to my feet, and announced clearly, "A toast—a toast to my wonderful husband."

"Emma," he said gently, noting some interest at the nearest tables, "perhaps you shouldn't."

"Please, let's dance," I said. "It's our wedding day."

I gave his hand a little tug. He stood and, with his arm around me, we walked to the empty dance floor. The music was soft and slow, and we danced as though we were one.

Suddenly the music changed to that lovely song from another generation, "I love you truly," and the crowd stood, clapping and shouting good wishes.

Charles bent his head to kiss me, but I turned my face. "You'll muss my hair." He laughed and kissed me anyway, then asked, "How do you think it's going to look in the morning?"

As it turned out, it looked as though it had never even had a passing acquaintance with a comb or brush, but as my hair lay across Charles's arm, he said it had never been so beautiful.

As soon as my feet hit the floor, I said, "Let's go home."

Charles said, "I checked out last night."

"A mind reader too," I teased.

I packed my lovely new things, with my wedding dress in the container in which it had been delivered, but wore my "foundation garment." The saleslady would have been proud of me.

After a hurried breakfast, Charles called for his car and we were on the road. The trip home seemed to pass quickly as we sped along, admiring the verdant green of the countryside and making plans for our future.

We stopped at a grocery store and, spying a nearby J.C. Penney store with a large sign that read "Jeans on Sale," I rushed in. "Old habits die hard," Charles called after me. "Get some that fit."

The big car purred along, eating up the miles. As we rounded the last curve, we saw the big house that seemed to be waiting for us. Charles's face was creased in a smile that stretched from ear to ear.

But when my little house, the one in which I had been born and spent most of my life, came into view, it looked so forlorn that a strong feeling of nostalgia swept over me. Charles, always sensitive to my moods, caught my feeling.

To hide my thoughts, I made a feeble joke. "My house or yours?"

His quick and firm answer: "Ours."

We had hardly closed the car doors behind us when we saw Mickey walking to meet us as fast as his legs could carry him. He was almost breathless.

"Mickey," Charles said, holding out my hand. "I want you to meet Mrs. Charles Halstad."

"Congratulations to you, my lady." His eyes twinkled and his feet danced a little jig. "That's the finest halter I've ever seen," he added as his eyes caught the sparkle of my ring.

Turning to Charles, he said, "What took you so long?"

We stood and chatted for a short while, and I asked Mickey, "Where are the girls?" I hadn't seen them in their usual pastures.

As though I had called her, an ear-splitting bray and the sound of her big hooves moving fast shattered the quiet. Charles and Mickey both stepped back quickly as she plowed to a stop and gently put her head on my shoulder, nudging, showing joy the only way she could at my return. I put my arms around her massive neck to keep my balance.

"That's more than sixteen hands of pure love," Mickey said, his voice thickening with emotion.

I felt my damp tears on her gray head so close to mine, and, uncaring of my new manicure, I scratched the place she liked best—the ear that was almost as long as her legs. Her other ear flicked back and forth as I whispered my love for her. I knew she loved me the same. The expression in those big dark eyes didn't lie.

A moment later, Charles's Birthday Girl and Babe, her rambunctious baby that had grown out of her foal stage, raced up the driveway. The long-legged devilish Babe kicking and bucking. I could almost hear Esmeralda thinking, little show-off.

Charles knelt between the two miniature donkeys while petting and talking, almost holding Babe in his arms.

Mickey laughed and said teasingly, "There you are, a grown man talking baby talk."

As he stood up brushing his pants, Charles promptly retorted, "I want to know why these girls are in the driveway."

Mickey sighed and rolled his eyes at me. "Your Esmeralda knocked down two fences, the board one, in two places. That was during the first two days you were gone. Then she tore up the wire fence. I don't know what she knocked down this time to be coming up the driveway. Tis Mrs. Halstad who's spoiled her," he laughed. "I'll just put them in your barn tonight."

"Our barn," Charles said.

"Perhaps I better put them away now," Mickey decided, "since I won't be here tonight." He walked away with Babe and Girl following. Ezzy waited for me.

"See what I mean?" Mickey called back as he watched Ezzy walk beside me. "Spoiled."

Then the battered old pickup sputtered down the road. Mickey's "See you tomorrow" grew fainter.

Charles and I walked up the steps of the veranda, and he fumbled with the keys as he unlocked the door. Reaching down suddenly, he scooped me up and carried me across the threshold. Still holding me, he said softly in my ear, "Madam, this is your domain," and put me on my feet. I was between laughter and tears.

The realization of his words took root. Through the window I saw my little house. Charles's eyes were on my face, waiting for my reaction.

It was now or never. With shaking knees, I stepped away. "The first thing I'm going to do is have that sofa bronzed and we will never part with it." The meaning of that outwardly frivolous declaration didn't escape Charles's quick mind. I knew I had to put his fears to rest.

"I love you, Emma," he said with his arms around me. "Let me show you your new home," he added, taking my hand and leading me from room to room.

The large master bedroom with the built-in dresser, the bath with its elaborate fixtures, the library a short walk down the hall. I thought of my treasured books packed away because my shelves were too crowded.

A lovely curving stairway to the upstairs bedrooms. "This was mine, the one across the hall was my brother's. He and Mother were both killed in an auto accident. If Dad were alive, I think he would be happy to know I've come home."

I thought my dad would have been happy too.

CHAPTER 10

Dawdling over our last cup of coffee the next morning, we watched the donkeys playing in the next pasture. Ezzy tolerated the frolicking mischievous Babe, who nibbled at the grand dame's tail. She seemed to have the patience of a grandmother. Laughing at their antics, our attention turned to our immediate future.

"Charles, I can't tell you how much I enjoyed our trip to Portland. There was so much to see and do—it was wonderful."

"Yes, especially the last part, "Charles teased. "You do remember that night, don't you?"

"My memory has improved," I said quickly, thinking back to the demeaning words I'd used after our night in the barn—"Couldn't have been much, I didn't remember it"—and the consequences.

Now it seemed so long ago and so much had changed. No longer was I an opinionated, ill-tempered old woman whose only interest in life upon awaking in the morning was worrying if the carrots had sprouted yet and what to do about those moles. I was just killing time before I joined the carrots.

Now this! I'm still seventy-five—the number on my birth certificate hasn't changed. But I'm not old—my heart is young and I'm alive for the very first time. And I'm going to savor every moment.

I threw my arms around Charles. "Oh, how I love you!"

My words ceased as he pulled me down on that sofa that had yet to be bronzed.

"You've never been old. I've always seen that green-eyed girl under the gray hair." He held me as we discussed future plans.

"Emma, I have worked all my life, never took time to travel, no hobbies. My one relaxation was in reading about someone else's pleasures. I always wanted to sail the seven seas," he laughed, "and see some of the world, but always my work took priority. I believe it's been the same with you. Let's take a cruise, a long one. I've given this a lot of thought and the time is now. What do you think?"

"A cruise? On a ship?" I was dazed by the sudden thought.

"Well, certainly not on a rowboat. Just think…just imagine…," his eyes danced with anticipation.

The sound of Mickey's pickup interrupted us as it labored up the driveway.

"Damn that Mickey," Charles exclaimed. "And he wonders why it took me so long to put that ring on your finger."

I held my hand out and admired my exquisite ring. "I'm glad you persevered."

Charles opened the door to Mickey's enthusiastic knock. With sparkling eyes and feet that would not stand still, he asked with a roguish grin, "Is it interrupting, I am? Charles, a word with you?"

They closed the door behind them, but I could hear their faint laughter. The door opened and Charles chuckled. "Mickey has a surprise for you in the barn."

We hurried to keep up with Mickey as he rushed to the old barn. There was Dad's ancient truck covered with dust, parked in the middle aisle, but past that stood a huge, brightly colored wagon. No, it couldn't be a wagon—it only had two wheels, wheels as tall as I, and a red velvet seat.

I sank down on the truck's dusty running board, breathless and almost in shock.

"What is it?"

"A driving cart for Ezzy. Make that donkey earn her keep," Mickey declared. "Charles ordered it custom-made. It arrived the day after you left."

Hanging on a peg where once had hung Dad's horse harness was enough leather to wrap up the entire barn.

"The most beautiful harness I've ever seen. Even the fancy horses I worked with in Ireland had nothing to compare," Mickey declared.

Charles sat down beside me and held my hand. "I thought you'd enjoy driving your famous donkey. You told me once that you'd driven your father's horses. Mickey would harness her for you."

I protested, "What will Ezzy think of this? She's old and retired, enjoying her old age." I could sense his disappointment in my lack of enthusiasm.

"She is in beautiful shape, her gray hair shines like silver in the sun. She's not done yet," Mickey said.

"Well, I may be. Haven't driven a wagon since I was sixteen and that's some years ago. Besides, the seat on that cart is so high I'd be halfway to heaven. How would I get in—or out?"

Quickly, I was shown the metal step. Charles suggested, "Why don't you bring her in? Let's hook her up and then see how you feel."

Reluctantly, I called Ezzy from the pasture and stood quietly as Mickey readied her for the cart. It was obvious he knew what went where. She waited patiently for the big, colorful cart to be hooked up as I followed Mickey's instructions to back her between the shaves. It seemed to me that she looked bored with it all.

Knowing Mickey was hoping to drive her, and since he had done most of the work, I thought it only fair to give him his wish. Besides, I was intimidated by the size of that cart.

Mickey stood on an old milk stool and crawled into the seat. The smile on his face as he lifted the reins was beatific. Looking down, his Irish brogue thickened. "Tis a magnificent animal, it tis." Then, in a firm voice, "Ezzy, move out, girl," and shook the reins.

Ezzy didn't even twitch an ear.

"Ezzy, move." She stood.

Mickey repeated loudly, "Ezzy, giddyup," and shook the reins vigorously with no response. After a few more vain attempts, he looked helplessly at us and said, "She's not gonna do it."

"Oh, for goodness sakes, get down. I'll drive her myself!"

With one foot on the step, the other on the ground, Mickey said, "Charles, she's just not going to do it. Guess she's tired of all that. I hope you can get your money back, at least for the harness. It can be cut down."

I interrupted. "Charles, will you please help me, now?"

Between the two of us, I was finally seated on the red velvet. I took the reins.

"Ezzy," I said with a gentle touch on the reins. "Walk." She moved with dignity, looking neither to the right nor the left and answering to the lightest touch.

We walked down the driveway to the road where we turned. I was delighted her ears picked up and she seemed to sense my pleasure. Another touch of the reins and a quiet "Move out, Ezzy" and her big body swung as gracefully as a dancer's into an effortless smooth trot. Little clouds of dirt drifted with each gigantic step. I was ecstatic.

I held the reins loosely—she seemed to know exactly what to do. I knew in her previous life that she had probably been trained by experts, so I was just along for the ride…and what a ride.

I didn't want to go back. What joy I felt to drive and see and hear and smell the great outdoors from my vantage point up high. After telling Ezzy how proud I was to be her driver, she lifted those hooves big as dinner plates and, with her head held high, almost pranced. The muted, nearly hypnotic sound in the soft dirt of the old road practically lulled me to sleep. What words could express the happiness that enveloped my whole being—a happiness that Charles's thoughtful, loving gift had given me.

At last we turned back to where I knew both Mickey and Charles were waiting. Charles looked at my radiant face as he helped me down.

"'Tis a monster you've created, Charles," Mickey said with a touch of envy. "This is going to take time from her baking."

After Ezzy was unharnessed, I stood at her head and scratched her ears, then walked her to the pasture where she rolled, shook herself, and trotted to join the others. As we headed to the house, I said, "Mickey, come in for some lemonade, and surely there's a piece of yesterday's pie."

"See?" Mickey said. "You've created a monster. I told you so."

"I know," Charles replied.

Since Mickey was no longer following his farrier trade, I suspected that he lived very frugally. But there were days when he indulged himself with a few cans of Pabst Blue Ribbon beer. Living by himself, I believed him to be a very lonely man. He and Charles had become fast friends. As I walked to the kitchen to perform my wifely duties, I looked back to see them sitting on the veranda, talking man talk with a can of something in their hands that wasn't lemonade. Mickey was always invited to lunch or dinner and regaled us with stories of his life in Ireland. Quick-witted and always with a joke, he became family to us.

Charles joked that we were adopting—at our age.

CHAPTER 11

I never tired of my time with Ezzy in the cart. Her gait was smooth and it was surprising to see just how fast her walking gait covered the ground. She seemed to enjoy it as much as I did.

As we finished our dinner one night, Charles asked, "What are your plans for that little house? Sell it? Rent it? Or are you just going to let it sit there and die?"

That question had been rolling around in my mind for a long time without an answer, but I certainly didn't plan to sell or rent it.

"Charles, what shall I do?"

"Your decision, my love."

A few more days passed and I could not bear to even look over—every board and shingle seemed to reproach me.

Then the solution flashed through my mind like a bolt of lightning.

At breakfast the next morning, I couldn't wait to tell Charles about my decision.

Before the coffee cooled, the words tumbled out.

"Charles, I've been thinking about our travel plans, and I think that Mickey should live in the little house. He'd take good care of it and good care of this one, too, when we travel. What do you think?"

"I'm delighted," he laughed as he pulled me down on his lap, coffee spilling all over my clean tablecloth. I had a sudden suspicion that that plan had already occurred to him.

Of course, Mickey was jubilant and couldn't wait to move in. His happiness brought tears to my eyes. Ezzy never had it so good. On second thought, none of us had ever had it so good.

Now that Mickey was here, Charles's enthusiasm for travel grew in leaps and bounds. Soon my interest joined his.

Then one day, Mickey went to town and came home with a poster announcing a three-day Fall Festival at the fairgrounds in a town about sixty miles away. It advertised all sorts of entertainment from Ferris wheels and cotton candy to black powder gun competition and various exhibitions. Mickey whooped with joy when, with his stubby finger, he highlighted the main attraction: a donkey trot race, cart required, on the quarter-mile track, with a five-hundred-dollar pot for the winner.

This was scheduled for next Friday, Saturday, and Sunday. His excitement was catching.

"Surely you are going to take Ezzy and show those amateurs what a real donkey can do," exclaimed Mickey.

Charles was hesitant. "I don't think you should do that, Emma. I know racing can get rough—it's very competitive, you know."

"Oh, but this is different," Mickey explained. "Just a bunch of the good old boys tryin' for the five-hundred-dollar jackpot, having fun."

Charles raised his eyebrows.

I allied myself with Mickey because I wanted to be a participant, not an observer, and to feel the excitement and the thrill of Ezzy winning her last race, as Mickey was sure she would.

"I could make a little money too—bets on the side, you know. And I have a plan." Mickey's eyes danced with devilment. "Friday, we will get Ezzy hooked. I will be in the seat, holding the reins. The missus will lead her to the starting line. I already will have made a lot of five-dollar bets that she will win by a head." He stopped for a breath then. "The starter gun will blow and they will all be off—except Ezzy. When the race is over, of course, they will torment me and I'll pay up." He turned to me. "Give you a chance to see who you have to beat."

Charles was not impressed.

Mickey wasn't through. "Saturday, of course, they are making fun of me and I tell them she'll run today, that she was just tired yesterday. So they are pleased to renew their bets and, of course, with the same results. And again I pay off. On Sunday, the big day, the missus will drive. I will bet she will win by a length and we'll win the pot."

Mickey was carried away with his plan, and we had to laugh with him as he had already spent his winning on repairs for the pickup. I could just see him out in the crowd bragging outrageously and trading insults. But the bottom line is that I wanted to do it—wanted to be more than just an onlooker. I knew Ezzy would win. Her last hurrah.

Charles went about with a long face while Mickey and I chattered like magpies. I hoped that when Charles saw the whole picture, he would look at things differently.

The following Thursday our caravan took off. Mickey had arranged for a trailer, which now had the cart securely strapped to the top and all essentials in place. It was difficult for even the three men who did the work under Mickey's critical eye. I led Ezzy in and she followed easily as though she, too, was anticipating this adventure.

A short time later we pulled into the fairgrounds and parked near the horse stalls. The men quickly unloaded the cart. We had kept the harness in the car for safekeeping. The passersby stood around admiring the oversized, colorful curiosity. I brought Ezzy out and the onlookers were astounded. Most people had never seen a mammoth donkey. She was comfortable in a large corner stall adjoining the stalls of her competitors.

The "good old boys," as Mickey called them, laughed and audibly commented that "The circus has come to town."

Mickey gave as good as he got. I wondered briefly if I should have listened to Charles.

The top door of Ezzy's stall was open and her big head almost filled it. Her ear-splitting bray quieted everyone momentarily.

Other donkeys were still being unloaded, and we saw that they were much smaller—"standard," someone said. Their carts were lined up by their stalls.

Everything was in order. Water and hay in Ezzy's stall. Mickey's sleeping bag and folding chair nearby. I knew he would not venture far from her.

The good old boys were sitting around drinking beer and telling tall tales. Little did they know that their competitor would make their stories sound like fairy tales. As we walked away, Mickey was in the midst of the rowdy group and they were laughing uproariously.

Charles and I found a nearby motel and a Big Mac for dinner. "I liked Portland better," groused Charles.

On Friday, at one in the afternoon, I was at Ezzy's head. Mickey, with a broad smile on his face, was sitting like a king on a throne holding the reins. His number was pinned to his back and he was in place. The other donkeys were restless, their drivers trying to hold them steady. I returned to the rail and stood with Charles.

The starting gun cracked and the donkeys streaked away, all jostling for the best position. Ezzy never even flinched at the sound of the gun or flicked an ear. She was bored. Her attitude seemed to be "been there, done that."

Mickey put on a realistic show with his shouting, bouncing up and down in the cart, pleading, waving the whip that was standard equipment—all to no avail. I walked out and led her back amidst the boos and ribald comments: "Get a horse." "Will she plow?"

I almost felt sorry for the feisty Irishman as he endured the ridicule heaped upon him. He just waved with a smug smile.

Saturday morning, Mickey bragged, "She'll run today. She was just tired yesterday."

"Wanna bet?"

The men gathered around. "You sure like to give your money away." "That donkey is so old she'll be lucky to live till she gets home."

And the betting was in full swing.

The Saturday race went exactly as Mickey had predicted. "You're just cluttering up the track," the winner said. "Why don't you go home."

Mickey paid up.

On Sunday morning I was up at five and urging Charles to hurry. "The race doesn't start till one. Why are you in such a big hurry?"

"Can't sleep and I want to be there."

Everyone was stirring down at the stalls. I groomed Ezzy to perfection and polished her harness. Charles urged me to have breakfast. Mickey hurried off to return with some stale donuts and coffee in paper cups. Coffee from a paper cup was not one of Charles's favorite things.

The winner of the last two races strutted around bragging about Payback, his donkey, and spitting Copenhagen. He was a big man with mean little eyes. It was easy to see he wasn't a favorite among the other drivers, who were edgy and tense and bordering on physical rebuttal. When he wandered over to our stall, I was glad that Charles had gone for more coffee.

"Why don't you go home, little man," he taunted Mickey. "We've got all your money."

"You haven't got all of it yet, you blowhard."

Mickey drew himself up to his full five feet eight inches and announced loudly, "Is there a big spender among you who will cover a real bet? I'll bet fifty dollars that my donkey will win this race by a length."

With that, he dug into his jeans, pulled out a fifty-dollar bill and waved it above his head.

Charles had returned with his coffee, which now spilled down the front of him.

"My god, he's lost his mind," a voice declared.

"Hell yes, sucker, I'll take your money."

The word spread like wildfire.

Mickey borrowed Charles's pen, walked to another building to pull a poster off the wall, and scribbled furiously on the back the names of all the men clamoring to take his money.

I could barely hear him say something about "see who will be crying at the end of this race," followed by his delighted laughter.

Charles laughed too. "I thought he was just trying for enough to buy new tires for the pickup, but now I believe it's a new truck he's after."

Then Mickey was back, his feet dancing, eyes squeezed shut with laughter. "Fifty dollars was all I had to my name," he said in a low voice.

Kissing Ezzy on the nose "for luck," Mickey said, "I know you won't stumble or I'll have to leave the country."

I helped Mickey harness my girl, not that he needed help, but I couldn't stand still. My heart was beating hard enough to break my ribs and sweat was dripping down my back. But I was ready.

Two stalls down, Payback was standing ready too.

"There's your only competition," Mickey muttered.

Payback's beady-eyed driver paused at our stalls and laughed. "Why don't you let grandma take the reins. She couldn't do any worse than you."

"That's a wonderful idea," Mickey said with a wink and a grin at me while pinning his number on my back.

"Charles, why don't you put her up."

"Oh, Emma, Emma," Charles groaned, "that's a rough bunch. Please reconsider."

"Put me up, Charles."

In a moment I was seated holding the reins as Mickey walked Ezzy to the lineup.

At the entrance, I was this little gray-haired woman holding the reins of the donkey that wouldn't run. Win or lose, I was the favorite.

Whistling, clapping, and cheering were followed by "Go, grandma, go!"

My excitement grew almost beyond containment.

There were six contestants. I was positioned third in line next to Payback's driver, and he was second to the rail. His driver looked up and said with an ugly laugh, "You'd better keep out of the way, grandma. You might get hurt."

Ezzy was ready. Her big ears were pointing straight ahead, and I could feel those big muscles tense.

The starting gun cracked. As the last note hung in the air, Ezzy's giant stride put her out in front.

Pandemonium raged in the bleachers. She kept the pace for a short time, then Payback worked his way around her and plowed his way to the rail. The bleachers were silent as though the watchers were holding their breath. The other drivers were strung out behind us. It was obvious that the race was between Ezzy and Payback.

It all seemed unreal to me—the wind blowing in my face, the dirt flying. Ezzy seemed to run with no effort, her powerful legs working like pistons. I could hear her steady, well-placed hoofs as they bit into the soft dirt. She was coming closer to her competitor with every powerful stride. Frothy lather was flying off Payback's body.

The roar of the crowd was clearly audible as we closed the gap—we were now neck and neck. Ezzy surged ahead, seemingly with no effort, and passed the laboring Payback. I made no attempt to guide her despite the fact that I held the reins. It was obvious that her training of years gone by had not abandoned her.

Ezzy pulled farther and farther ahead. Hearing the driver behind me cursing and belaboring his exhausted donkey, I waved bye-bye and threw him a kiss as we thundered over the finish line—winners by two lengths.

The track was a scene of wild confusion. We were surrounded by a sea of humanity. Mickey ran to throw his arm around Ezzy's neck and his tears flowed. I slid down into Charles's arms. His eyes were wet. "Thank God you're safe. You were magnificent. I am so proud of you."

Together we pushed our way to Ezzy's head. She gave a mighty sigh and lay her head on my shoulder. My tears rivaled Mickey's.

A news photographer took my picture holding a five-hundred-dollar check and a fancy trophy. We were front-page news.

Struggling through the crowd, we made our way to Ezzy's stall and Charles and I managed to unhitch her and take off her harness. Mickey was still at the track collecting his bets. We wiped her sweaty sides and dusty face and walked to cool her off while we waited for the little entrepreneur.

Four of the other drivers came over to congratulate me. One of them said, "You'll notice the empty stall. Payback was loaded and gone as soon as you hit the finish line. Good riddance too."

Charles said, "That was a good move and I think we should do the same."

"Yes," I said. "Let's go home. Where is Mickey?"

Almost on cue, he came walking past the stalls holding a greasy cap tightly in his hand. He handed it to me with an indescribable look, said "Take care," and went to find the haulers. I shook the greasy thing and heard distinctly the rattle of silver and the soft rustle of paper.

We picked up our few belongings at the motel and followed the trailer home. Mickey sat in the back seat counting his money.

"How much, Mickey?" I asked.

He said, "Ask the banker how much thirty times fifty is, not counting the IOUs."

Charles started to laugh and it was infectious. I opened my purse and handed Mickey the five-hundred-dollar check. At last Mickey seemed at a loss for words.

Charles broke the silence when he asked, "Mickey, that wasn't quite honest, was it?"

"Well," he answered quite logically, "they were happy to take my money, so why shouldn't I be happy to take theirs?"

"That does seem reasonable when you look at it that way," Charles agreed, and again the car rocked with laughter.

CHAPTER 12

It was good to be home. Ezzy was quickly unloaded and ran to meet Birthday Girl and Babe, who raced to meet her halfway.

It was satisfying to be in our own bed again, and sleep came quickly in the quiet country.

The next morning I gave Ezzy the rest she so richly deserved, then concentrated on my baking crusty loaves of bread and apple pies.

Mickey, who was mowing lawns and fixing fences, was easily lured to the house by the aroma of apple pies. The pie had already been reduced by half when Charles's quick action saved him the last three pieces. He leaned back in his chair, observing, "Coffee sure tastes better in a China cup."

We sat around the table talking about the festival and Mickey's good fortune at the races.

"What are you going to do with all that money?" I asked.

"Count it," he answered promptly. "Every night. I've never had my hands on that much money in my life."

"What are you going to do with that big trophy?" He pointed to where it stood in the center of the table.

"Remember how hard Ezzy worked for it? I'm going to hang it in her stall."

I never regretted Mickey's stay at my house. He took better care of it than I had. He took charge of everything that needed to be done outside—no more hard labor for me. My fingernails grew long enough to scratch Ezzy's ears until she closed her eyes and sighed with deep pleasure.

Then, too, either I gained weight or my jeans had shrunk. I was flattered beyond words when Charles said I had the figure of a young girl. Knowing better, of course, but hearing those words from the man I loved made me feel sixteen again.

Charles hadn't gotten past his desire to travel, but my mind was focused on a plan for the winter garden. I hoped he'd forget about ships and countries halfway across the world. I was comfortable at home, and I tried to forget that we had made all the arrangements for our passports just after we married.

In the coming weeks, the trees were already starting to turn color, and I was planning the winter garden in my mind. Standing at the window gazing out, I could see the climbing roses that Mickey had planted at the little house were now starting to fade. I saw the almost translucent smoke drifting upwards, and I knew he had built a fire in the old kitchen stove and was making mulligan stew.

The thought occurred to me that the autumn of our lives had far outdistanced our spring and that if we didn't have a dime, we would still be rich. My reverie was broken by

Charles's exuberant voice. "Emma, Emma. This is it—look, this is the one!"

He was waving a vividly colored magazine that had appeared after he had returned from town. We sat on the sofa, and he turned the pages until he came to the one on which the heading read in large block print, "Transatlantic Cruise, a cruise of Western Europe for four weeks."

"Four weeks? That's a long time, Charles. What about our animals and …"

"We have Mickey here to care for them, so why worry about the time?"

In his mind he was already walking the deck and breathing the salt air. My plans for a winter garden suddenly became nonexistent.

Turning the page, we learned that it was a five-star luxury ship that would sail in three weeks out of Fort Lauderdale, Florida.

Already his mind had jumped three weeks ahead.

"We will fly to Fort Lauderdale and board the Miramar there. This cruise promises every luxury and we deserve that. We are at the right age to enjoy the good times and plan for more of the same in the future."

His happiness radiated from every pore.

"Just imagine, Emma."

How could I? I'd never been out of Oregon.

"We could explore Europe at all the ports of call," and he read off the list. "We could wander the streets of Lisbon, Portugal, and see Ponta Delgada. And visit the pubs in Dover, England." He stopped to catch his breath; his face flushed with excitement. "A canal cruise in Holland, then a tour of the ancient French castle, Chateau de Balleroy, plus all the wonderful things to do on board. Oh, Emma, say you'll be as happy as I am."

I was wordless. My mind couldn't wrap around such an incredible event. The lie fell out of my mouth as I hedged, "Of course, I'm happy." But the truth was, I was scared to leave what I had always known and less than thrilled about traveling halfway across the world. What's so great about an old, decaying castle?

He sensed my reluctance. I felt his disappointment and was ashamed to tarnish his joy with my schoolgirl fears and cool responses. So even if it meant my demise, I was determined to be happy.

I could have gone on the stage—my performance was star quality as I tried to be happy happy happy. In the days to come, a subtle change crept over me as Charles's enthusiasm bubbled over and swept me along. And I saw through his eyes the windmills and tulips in Holland and could almost smell the musty old Balleroy castle. My heart beat faster at the thought of us walking hand in hand down the colorful streets of Lisbon. Charles said that he could already taste the beer in Dover.

We talked late into the night. Each day seemed to hurry by as we prepared.

"Don't worry about a thing," Charles said. "I already have the tickets. Luggage? I have enough for both of us. Bring what you'd like, but they have shops on board where you can find anything you need. We'll fly from Portland to Fort Lauderdale and we'll board the ship there."

I thought he was going to burst with excitement.

Every day some time was spent with Ezzy. Her head was always on my shoulder as I told her what a great girl she was and how I would miss her and promised to be home soon. Charles was spending time with his girls too.

My feelings were comforted knowing that Mickey would give all our animals the best of care.

When we told Mickey about our plans, he snorted, "England? You've missed your mark. Now Ireland, that's where you'll find the best pubs in the world."

He was both happy and sad, and I knew he'd miss the companionship that we all enjoyed. Our announcement seemed to give him the incentive to part with his money, and shortly he indulged himself with a shiny new red pickup. Laughing, he teased, "This is my cruise and it will last longer than four weeks."

"Probably so," Charles answered, "but our memories will last forever."

CHAPTER 13

At last the magic day dawned. We had driven to Portland the day before and stayed at the same hotel we had enjoyed previously, where Charles garaged the car. We were up far earlier than necessary and had a quick breakfast, then took a cab to the airport where Charles checked our luggage through to Fort Lauderdale with the comment, "I hope they don't lose it."

This only added to my anxiety on my maiden flight. Obviously Charles had been a frequent flyer during his banking career.

The airport was crowded. So many people pushing, shoving, moving in every direction. It seemed that the entire population of Portland was trying to catch a flight.

Despite the fact that I put on a brave front in the safety of my own home, when faced with the reality, my courage faltered. My knees shook and I grasped Charles's hand as though I were drowning. Charles gave me a pep talk that would have inspired the Forty Niner football team, and concluded with, "Relax, Emma. Relax, we're having fun."

Shortly after the preliminaries were over, we boarded a little plane. As Charles urged me to a window seat, I was astounded to count only eighteen people.

"It's a commuter plane," he explained. "Wait until you see the one in San Francisco."

I closed my eyes and tried to compose myself. Daring to open them, it was to see the city disappear. The soft fleecy clouds drifted by to cover snowy mountaintops. I was entranced to see civilization so far below. We had hardly gotten comfortable when the misty outlines of San Francisco appeared.

The San Francisco International Airport terminal made Portland look like a pit stop. The enormous planes were unreal. Of course, I had read about jumbo jets but had no interest in anything but my own little world.

The commuter plane looked like a sparrow that had accidentally flown into an eagle's convention. We went through the various preliminaries again, but the lines were longer and we were in a sea of surging, crowding humanity. With me clinging to Charles's arm, we pushed our way to our boarding gate, exhausted by the noise and the effort it took to get us to the last stop of our journey by air.

Waiting, we were fascinated by the diversity of the countless people coming and going endlessly and knew we were already far from home.

When the flight was called, we joined a line that seemed to have no end and rushed to push into the plane—a plane that appeared to me to be as long as a football field—that filled slowly but surely with boisterous travelers.

Charles led me to a deep, comfortable seat next to a window and settled himself beside me. I closed my eyes and tried to remember that this was the last part of our air adventure.

People were still loading when I opened my eyes, shocked to see we were high in the air, but the plane hadn't left the ground.

Charles laughed at me. "A few more of these trips and you'll be a seasoned traveler."

I closed my eyes again as a frightening thought raced through my mind: Heaven help me. He's already planning another trip and we're still stationary.

The buzz of conversation quieted as the big plane lifted into the air. The noise of the wheels retracting made me certain that we were about to crash. I squeezed my eyes tightly shut.

Charles said, with just a hint of irritation, "Are you going to be blind this entire trip, Emma?"

His words jolted me, and I leaned closer to the window to see the city disappear back into the mist and was awestruck when I saw the mountaintops, the canyons, and the prairies that stretched so far.

Charles told me that it would be about a six-hour flight and that our cruise ship was considered a small, even though it carried eighteen hundred passengers.

We were settled in soft, deep seats, as comfortable as any chair in our home. From where we sat, we could hardly hear the voices of our fellow passengers.

"First Class," Charles said. "I travel only in First Class. We need to be comfortable." And I surely was.

Charles buzzed for the flight attendant and ordered lunch. It was just as good as he said it would be. Already it had been a long day, and I was full of good food and grew drowsy. Leaning back, the song of the engines lulled me to sleep.

It seemed such a short time that I'd slept when Charles awakened me. "We're about twenty minutes out—don't you want to see?"

The plane was dropping to lower altitudes and Charles squeezed beside me. Together we saw the tropical lay of the land. Lower still, we saw the outline of the big city and beyond it the azure blue of the ocean with ships crowding the harbor. My breath caught with the magnificent sight.

The plane rolled to a smooth stop, and we followed along with the rest of the pleasure-bent travelers through a corridor that connected the plane to the terminal.

At the exit stood a man holding a large sign that read, "Miramar." We joined the group that gathered around him and soon were transported in a very crowded shuttle bus to a lovely hotel, where we spent the night to wait for the return of the bus to pick us up at two in the afternoon the next day. The bus would take us to the ship—the ship that would carry us on our journey that Charles had spoken of with endless delight for weeks. And now his dream was becoming reality.

We had dinner that night with our fellow travelers, all from various states—only Charles and I were from Oregon. We slept well and had an early breakfast.

Today was the day we embarked, and we impatiently waited for the bus. When it arrived, it was filled almost before it stopped. It emptied even more quickly when we reached the embarkation site.

It was then that I saw the ship close up. It seemed as big as a small city. My eyes were almost blinded by the beauty of it. Long sleek lines from bow to stern, white as though the Lord has given one majestic sweep of His brush, omitting only the lifeboats, which were detailed in bright colors and clung to her like a necklace.

Hundreds of people milling about, it was a kaleidoscope of color. The luggage was piled high, the workmen were scurrying around to load everything. Somewhere music was playing and I could see young people dancing and hear whoops of laughter—everyone was trying to talk above the din. An aura of happiness and goodwill seemed to weld us together.

Already Charles was making friends, shaking hands, joking, and somehow we got separated. Unexpectedly, a gray-haired lady put her arm around my shoulder and shrieked, "Isn't this hilarious? Are we having fun yet?" She swung me around and did a little dance. We joined hands, giggling like teenagers and danced the way we did when we were young.

From somewhere a voice was heard. "Will you look at those two old ladies swing it?"

"They are not 'old ladies.' They are two girls having some fun," came another voice.

That was so true—more fun than I ever could have imagined.

When Charles found us, his eyes widened and he threw back his head and laughed as I had never heard him. Joining us, he never missed a step until at last, gasping for breath, we stopped. The woman stuck out her hand and said, "Mattie," and added, "Those kids have got it, but we old gals had it first."

"Emma," I answered and collapsed against Charles.

It felt like centuries ago that I had planted a spring garden, and fought moles and gophers. In reality, it was how many months?

Back then I was content to sit in my big chair watching the fire in the old stove, thinking that my life was complete. Now I am thousands of miles away from that old stove, dancing with a stranger on the asphalt. I felt like Alice falling down the rabbit hole.

Lines of people were passing through the security building presenting their passports and other documents, then passing over the short connecting bridge to step into the ship. We were almost carried along by the stampede when we found ourselves next in line. Charles was in charge and I had no need to be nervous, so I attributed the trembling of my knees to the excitement. We were soon cleared and waved on.

As we stepped across the threshold of this tremendous ship, a thrill ran up my back at the luxurious interior—even Charles was impressed.

"Let's go to the top deck and see ourselves off," Charles said, so we took the first elevator available. In a matter of moments, we stepped out to join the horde of revelers crowding the rail, shouting, blowing kisses and waving to the well-wishers from our vantage point so high above.

The ship's departure whistle blared, and I felt the massive engines as they engaged the powerful propellers. Slowly the ship moved out into deeper water and soon the city faded into the horizon. The deck quickly emptied as the passengers wandered off to explore their surroundings.

"Let's stay awhile," Charles suggested. "It's so quiet. This is just for us."

Standing hand in hand at the rail, we watched the endless ocean—so blue it was almost purple—seem to melt into the sky. The quiet lengthened. It seemed that we were alone and quite unnecessary in this vast universe.

I turned my head and watched the blue-green waves with their canopies of froth that hung so quickly. I closed my eyes and felt the power of the determined waves as they pushed themselves against the giant ship's passage—as if to challenge her right to share that vast expanse of ocean. I heard the call of a lonely sea gull as it followed.

I shivered, and Charles put his arm around me and pulled me close.

Now the sounds of revelry and music drifted up to us and with it the aroma of something delicious.

"Let's go down," Charles said. "It must be dinnertime, and tomorrow is another day."

The second night out we were seated with the other festive celebrants at the Captain's table. We didn't eat; we dined. It wasn't food, but cuisine unlike anything I ever could have imagined.

Looking around the table at beautifully gowned women and their escorts, I felt like Cinderella at the ball. But in my heart I knew that when the clock struck midnight I would still be Cinderella with my handsome, silver-haired prince holding my hand under the table.

Later Charles found the casino and I browsed the fancy shops. He gave me his winnings with the words, "My dear, buy yourself a present."

The sapphire and diamond ring that sparkled on my finger looked perfect with my blue dress. Looking down at my hand as it lay on Charles's arm, I smiled. Did these fingers ever bury themselves in bat guano or scratch a donkey's ears, or have they always been soft and white, the nails perfectly manicured? Only the slight crook in my left thumb betrayed a previous life.

Our stateroom was large and luxurious, opening onto a balcony where we often had tea in late afternoon. We watched the frothy waves and then the sun as it disappeared below the horizon, releasing to the darkness the shimmering golden rays that danced on the water.

Warm against the comfort of Charles's back, I sometimes awakened in the night to hear the steady throb of the engines and the constant swish of the waves against the prow. We were a thousand miles from everywhere and I cuddled closer.

The ports of call were everything the brochure declared. In Holland we floated down one of the many canals on a boat that almost rivaled our ship, mingling with the exotic mix of tourists in a world never imagined as I weeded in my garden or nailed up a loose screen.

The beer in Dover made me tipsy. Charles laughed and held my arm. Then there was Lisbon, with its colorful cobbled streets, magnificent historical buildings, its exuberant people. The century-old Balleroy Castle in Normandy was almost frightening in its grim exterior. The scent of mildew still clings to the shoes I wore that day.

Then it was time to come home. Lifting my glass to Charles, I said, "Next year, let's go again, and this time my choice. I think the Greek Isles."

"Done," he exclaimed and lifted his glass to mine.

CHAPTER 14

Ah, it was good to be home. So very good. The fall weather was fast approaching but still warm and beautiful, nudging Mickey and Charles to start plans for a big garden, plans that didn't include me. It felt strange—all these years it had been my garden.

I was an outdoor woman. Housework had never been my priority. However, when I was hot and sweaty and my back was killing me, alternatives came to mind. I had promised myself that someday, when I retired, I was going to create a cookbook, combining Mother's award-winning recipes with grandma's handed-down favorites. And just for fun, I'd include directions for Mickey's mulligan stew, that is if mere words could even describe it. Perhaps I was retired and the realization hadn't reached me yet.

Breakfast was over and Mickey had departed. Charles was on his last cup of coffee.

Putting on my boots, I stepped out on the veranda to meet the sunshiny morning. Resisting with much effort the urge to sit on the veranda steps and just enjoy the beauty, I paused at the potted petunias that lined the railing, their beauty just beginning to fade. I stuck a finger into the soil, finding it very dry, then walked around the corner to the peonies that long since had given up their spectacular blooms in preparation for winter. They, too, needed water.

I uncoiled the water hose from its rack and turned the water on full force, soaking the thirsty plants. Above the sound of the water I heard an unidentifiable shriek. Tanzy, our mail carrier, was running up the driveway screaming and waving her arms like a windmill. Up the steps she sprinted. Charles must have heard her—he stood at the open door and she rushed inside.

I thought she was probably asking about Mickey's whereabouts, but what an entrance. What is she so excited about? Has she won the jackpot or does she just like the attention? Any woman who delivers mail in her shorts…

What's keeping her? Waiting for her to come out, I continued watering, even over the railing to reach the flower beds below. My thoughts wandered: I wonder if that red hair is natural. Seems a little dark at the roots.

I moved closer to the door to catch the petunias there and soaked them until the water cascaded down the sides of the pot and ran over my boots. She's been in there long enough for Charles to draw her a map.

I was becoming increasingly irritated—what are they doing? Having coffee? My anger smoldered, then broke into a blind fury upon hearing her high-pitched, slurred words,

"Oh, Charles, hurry, hurry." I pushed open the door, the gushing hose in my hand forgotten.

My disbelieving eyes saw Tanzy in my chair, her head tilted back, resting on the top as if inviting a kiss.

I heard her muted, "Oh, hurry, hurry" as Charles's face bent over hers, one hand in her hair.

All reason left me.

I lifted the hose and hit her with a stream of water that almost knocked her out of the chair, then turned the hose on Charles.

She shoved past me and ran screaming down the driveway. Shocked, Charles yelled, "Emma, stop. Emma!"

I did—abruptly, because the water had been cut off.

Looking over my shoulder I saw Mickey's horrified face. I seethed at Charles as he spoke for a brief moment with Mickey, then they both hurried to the truck and raced down the driveway to overtake Tanzy.

I watched in a stifled rage as Charles got out and helped her into the truck. Then they sped away.

I surveyed my once spotless kitchen with dissatisfaction. Broken coffee cup, chair overturned, water dripping from the curtains. The floor slick and wet.

Leaving a sloppy trail as I walked to our bedroom, I collected my pillow, some dry clothes, and personal things I would need until I could get back in my old house.

The tumultuous feelings, held at bay, started to flow as I walked down the path, but I ground them away with the back of my hand.

Slumping down on the back step of my little house and looking up at the house where I had known great happiness, the sick hurt that boiled in my entire being begged for release. Finally, the scalding tears traced a salty line down a wrinkle that I hadn't noticed yesterday. Apparently other things that should have been fairly obvious had gone unnoticed. I berated myself.

Why hadn't I listened to my common sense in the beginning? Knowing from the start that we were from different worlds, how could I have been so blind? Old enough to know better, I should have known it was too good to be true.

How could he?

That Tanzy floozy—I should have drowned her.

Mickey did not come home that night and I did not turn on the lights. I watched to see the lights come on in Charles's study, but the room darkened so quickly that I may have imagined it.

Pulling a blanket from the bed in the spare bedroom, I got as comfortable as possible on my old lumpy sofa, thinking This is not as cozy as the big one I had last slept on how many eons ago.

Mickey drove in late the next morning. I saw him and Charles sitting on the veranda steps deep in conversation.

Yesterday morning we had lingered over coffee, hot cakes, and good bacon in my pretty kitchen. Now I was eating stale toast and wondering how this was going to be resolved. One thing for sure is I am never going back to that house. Let Tanzy clean up the kitchen. She seemed so comfortable.

Inwardly raging at the vision, I hated them both.

Holding my old battered coffeepot, searching for coffee, I heard a quick knock on the door and looked over to see

Mickey standing in the doorway. We looked at each other without speaking. Over his shoulder I saw the truck. Then he glanced at the sofa with a raised eyebrow.

"I trust you slept well, Mrs. Halstad." The tone of his voice didn't sound like Mickey.

I didn't answer, but continued to open drawers.

"If you're looking for coffee, you won't find any. You surely remember we always have coffee at your house in the morning. I'd like you to take a little ride with me. I need to show you something."

Irritably I answered, "Mickey, can't it wait? I've got other plans."

"Please, Mrs. Halstad, this won't take much of your time and I wouldn't ask you if it wasn't important."

I gave a disgusted sigh and resigned myself, walked past him and got into the truck.

As we drove down the driveway, the truck stopped. Charles appeared from nowhere and slid in without a word.

"Mickey," I said angrily, "stop the truck. I am not going anywhere with this Romeo."

I pushed against Charles. He acted as if I wasn't there. The truck picked up speed.

"Where are you taking me and why?"

"Just a few miles down the road. Nine, to be exact, and then you will be home as soon as you like," Mickey said tersely.

I sat in sullen silence.

The truck slowed, then turned up a short dirt road and stopped at a prim little white-frame house that seemed to be partly unroofed. The truck stopped; we sat a moment.

There was no sign of activity—everything seemed too quiet. I would have thought it vacant, but there were red geraniums blooming in a window box below the white curtains that fluttered in the opening.

"Mickey," I said emphatically. "I am not getting out of this truck until you tell me why I've been practically abducted."

For the first time, Charles spoke. "Yes, you are going to get out of this truck." His cold, unfamiliar voice told me I was going to get out willingly or otherwise.

Mickey got out and was greeted as an old friend by a dog slowly wagging its tail. Charles was holding the door for me, waiting expectantly. I waited as long as I dared, then reluctantly stepped out.

Mickey walked ahead. I followed slowly, sensing Charles's presence behind me.

Mickey paused at the door, seeming a bit hesitant. Then, giving a quick knock, he waited for me to enter. Instinctively I stepped back. This didn't feel right, but Charles stood solidly behind, then took my arm and guided me in.

It took a moment for my eyes to adjust, then I turned my head to the wheezing sound that came from a seated woman with her back to us. In the dead silence of the room, her labored breathing seemed to reverberate off the walls.

"Tanzy, I've brought Mrs. Halstad to see you."

As he spoke, Mickey walked to her and turned the chair to face me. Her head lifted and I gasped in horror at the grotesque mask that was her swollen face.

One eye swelled tightly shut, just a slit of color showed in the other. Nose and mouth merged together. Her red hair stuck out at different angles as though that too had not escaped the devastation.

Mickey moved to adjust the light cotton robe that had been thrown over her as if she could not bear the touch of anything on that tortured flesh. A deformed hand with fingers thick and splayed lay in her lap.

She looked up at me as I stood before her and attempted to speak, but the words were unintelligible from that distorted mouth.

My mind vainly sought an answer. Why? Why have I been brought here? I've had no part in this terrible happening. All I did was splash a little water on her. I tried to turn away, but I felt Charles's hands on my back.

"Let me say it for you, Tanzy," came Mickey's gentle voice. Tears squeezed from her blind eyes as she nodded. He turned to me.

"She said she is so sorry to have upset you, Mrs. Halstad, and asked you to forgive her, that she didn't mean to cause you trouble." Mickey's voice shook.

I stood dumbfounded, not understanding.

"Let me tell you," said Mickey, his voice toughening, "what happened yesterday. Tanzy was delivering the mail as usual when we're guessing she dropped something. She must have stooped to pick it up, and, as she stood, her head bumped into a big yellow-jacket nest on the back of the mailbox. Part of it is still hanging there. The weeds are high along that ditch and thick around the post. That's why we've never noticed the nest.

"Now, Tanzy is deadly allergic to stings. I'm sure you know about anaphylactic shock. She must have run to her car for the kit she always carried because we found it on the road—it had expired.

"She knew it would be a very short time before she lost consciousness, so she ran up the driveway to see me and found Charles. He, not knowing of her allergy, attempted to pull the stingers out with tweezers. She ran back down the driveway to escape you—perhaps that saved her life because I saw her then, but it also spread the poison faster. Thank God we got her to the emergency room without a moment to spare—she was unconscious. The doctor pumped her full of antidotes and hooked her up to the oxygen for a couple of hours. He said the swelling and pain would be gone in a week or so, and told her not to be careless about her kit. She might not be so lucky next time. I stayed with her last night and kept the ice packs moving."

The enormity of my actions seared me to my very soul. She had come for help, death riding on her shoulders, and because of my groundless jealousy, I had almost pushed her into the grave.

The horror registered and I fell to my knees, crying hysterically from shame and guilt.

Her arm reached for me and those swollen splayed fingers brought me to her. I lay my head in her lap. Our tears intermingled, exchanging words that neither of us understood, but with perfect understanding. That incredible gift of forgiveness that she so freely gave to me, I never forgot. And in her big, generous heart, she never remembered.

Charles almost lifted me to my feet into his waiting arms.

Mickey wiped her face tenderly, adjusted an ice pack, then turned to say, "Don't cry, Mrs. Halstad, she will get better." I knew then that he had forgiven me too.

Raising my face from Charles's shirtfront I asked him, "Can we take her home so I can care for her?"

He looked over my shoulder as my question hung in the air. Tanzy nodded. The men left to bring the truck.

I catered to her every need—bathing her daily, applying soothing ointment day and night, easing the pain—until the swelling gradually receded. Shampooing and brushing that tangle of hair, I found it red to the roots with only a few strands of gray. While bathing her it was obvious there was no cellulite as my jealous mind imagined, even hoped for, and the breasts were her own.

I turned my eyes away as if to rid myself of the realization that I had been capable of such petty meanness. I don't know if it was my desperate need to make amends or my good nursing care, but royalty never had it any better.

The doctor was surprised at Tanzy's quick recovery, but I knew she was on the mend when she bedeviled Mickey by patting the bed beside her and suggesting that he join her and "take my temperature."

Even his ears were red, but that didn't deter his daily visits.

A week later Tanzy and I were having after-breakfast coffee in the kitchen, she comfortable in Charles's robe.

Looking across the table I could imagine the beautiful girl she must have been even though she seemingly retained much of her beauty. She was not modest or shy, but outspoken, quick-witted, and not above a bawdy joke. She swept me along with her—I was surprised at myself as I looked forward to our "kitchen breaks," our time to get acquainted, which seemed to ripen quickly into a real friendship.

"I must go home," she said, but I insisted, "No, you must stay awhile," with the feeble excuse that made us both laugh: "You might have a relapse. Send Mickey to your house for your clothes."

"Can't you just see him digging through my panty drawer?" she hooted. And we giggled like schoolgirls.

But she did stay another week, and by then I felt that we were close friends for a lifetime. Charles enjoyed her, too, and Mickey positively glowed.

The breakfast dishes were done and the kitchen tidied up. Tanzy was going home tomorrow. I felt a sudden pang. "I'm going to miss you, Tanzy. You are the closest friend I've ever had."

She gave me a quick hug and said, "I can return the compliment."

Did I hear a catch in her voice? Half embarrassed by our show of sentiment, I said quickly, "I'll put on the coffee and you can tell me the story of your life. How did you become a mail carrier?"

"Believe me," she laughed, "I took the long way around."

We pulled our chairs up to the table that had endured our every morning conversations and confidences that I had never shared with anyone else, waiting for a moment as she seemed to hesitate.

"I had a miserable childhood. Tall, skinny, redheaded— not a winning combination. My father wanted a son so badly, but what my mother presented him with was this girl who was taller at fifteen than he was. I was taller than my teacher too.

The kids at school bullied me unmercifully, and I developed an inferiority complex up to here," she said, raising her arm. "I became very antisocial too."

She paused and looked off into space as though remembering. After I refilled her coffee cup, she sipped and continued.

"When I graduated high school, Dad boarded up the house and said, 'Move to town, get a job, girl, there's enough money to keep you a couple of weeks. Be sure to keep the taxes up; you may want this house someday.'

"My folks moved back east and I moved to Portland, to a rooming house that I could afford. Barely eighteen, this country girl was terrified of the big city, but excited and looking for a job to pay the taxes. I wasn't trained for anything. Mother had taught me to sew a little so I answered an ad for a seamstress' helper, thankfully starting the job just as my money ran out.

"On my first day of work, a door was opened to a big, dimly lit theater with rows and rows of seats. The marquee read 'The Golden Slipper.' All the action was on the brightly lit stage where the music was blaring and a line of girls dancing.

" 'No, no, no, not like that. Somebody turn the damn music off,' a man yelled while waving his arms. 'You, you over there,' he pointed, 'have you got any sense of rhythm? How long have we been rehearsing this? You better be thinking about picking up your check.'

"The poor girl ran off the stage, screaming curses and crying. The line broke up and the dancers milled around the man, who was now dancing and yelling, 'Like this, like this! Is that so damn difficult?'

"I stood petrified. Finally some man noticed me. Taking my arm, he led me backstage and opened a door. 'The cleaning stuff is in there,' he said, 'start with the toilets.'

"But, but," I stuttered, and he repeated, 'Start with the toilets,' and gave me a little push."

"Tanzy, you didn't," I voiced in shock.

"Well, the landlady wanted her money," she shrugged.

"I had been working there about a year and the toilets never shined brighter. In addition, I was the gofer for everyone from the maintenance man to the dancing girls. I never saw a needle.

"Despite the hard work, I came back at night to see the show. The girls, so ordinary at rehearsals, transformed into beautiful sequined performers as if a magic wand had touched them. The music, lights, dancing girls, and the cloudy smoke-filled auditorium beyond the stage—I loved it all. I had never been happier in my life. I would have worked for nothing—I felt like a sparrow caught up in a peacock's fantasy."

I saw through Tanzy's eyes what I had never seen with my own.

"Am I boring you?"

"No, no. Go on, don't stop now."

"Then one day I was stretched to my full extent reaching for some hat boxes on a high shelf when I heard the voices of two men who were walking by. They paused behind me for a few minutes and I could feel their eyes on me. Then one said, 'Look at those legs. They go all the way to heaven. They'd make kindling out of that pole.'

" 'She's got a nice ass too,' the other voice added. 'Hey, you! Turn around,' he said as he pulled the pins from my hair, which fell almost to my waist. 'Not hard to look at even in those clothes.' They talked as though I was an inanimate object. 'What do you think?' 'I think she's a natural.'

" 'Hey, can you dance?'

" 'No,' I whispered.

" 'We'll send you to Georgie and he'll make you a star.'

"And that's exactly what happened.

"I was nineteen and under the tutelage of Georgie, who took me in hand and taught me how to walk. 'Stand up straight, straight. Hold your head up. Don't walk, strut like you own the world. You do, you know. There isn't a woman here who has what you've got—youth, beauty and all put together in the right places. Flirt with your audience, make each one think he is the only man in the world and that you will be waiting for him.'

"Oh, yes, Georgie taught me all the angles and I was an apt pupil. Just one night on the stage and I was no longer a shy country girl, but a dancer in a costume smaller than a man's handkerchief, with wild hair flying, a leg wrapped around the pole, every sequin winking, flirting with a sea of yelling, clapping, laughing men who threw lots of money at me. At last I found my niche; I was accepted."

"Tanzy," I interrupted, or tried to. But she was into her story and gave me that devilish smile that I had seen before when she walked up Charles's driveway.

"There was one man who came every Wednesday and Saturday and sat in the second row," Tanzy continued. "Black curly hair that I would have loved to run my fingers through, for starters. I flirted with all of them, but my eyes always came back to him. Strange, I never knew him, but I never forgot him. He was always gone when my act was over. The show moved to Seattle and I never saw him again. Now, forty years later, I meet him on a dirt road beside a mailbox." She whooped with laughter, "Isn't that incredible?"

I could only nod wordlessly.

My concentration was broken by a quick knock and Mickey stepped in. "I picked up your mail today, Tanzy," he said as he tossed a letter on the table. Then he was gone. Mickey always arrives at the most inopportune moments, I thought.

"Probably just junk mail. Go ahead and toss it—I never get anything but the tax bill."

"Go on, Tanzy," I urged.

She looked thoughtful. "Maybe I can sell my story to True Confessions. Then I could have the roof shingled. I'd stay dry this winter and…"

"Go on, Tanzy, go on. Don't leave me hanging," I begged.

"Well," she began, "I stayed with the show for about ten years, until I was weary of the whole scene. Then I took my savings and did what I had often thought—dreamed, even— of doing. I traveled in Europe and spent time in Madrid where I made scores of acquaintances, but no one special. Well, there was a man there who taught me to tango," she smiled that smile again. "And I taught him some new steps too."

I looked away. Hers was not a story borrowed from *Grimm's Fairy Tales*.

"When my money ran out I came back to Portland and worked for years as a saleslady for some of the best stores. But I got tired of that world and came back to the house I'd paid taxes on for forever, it seemed. It was a disaster. Blackberry vines and weeds had overrun most of the forty acres. I'd like to sell part of it.

"Mickey has been helping with those vines, but he sure doesn't enjoy that line of work. The thorns are an inch long and the vines can trip you. I take him a tuna sandwich at lunch and a couple cans of cold beer. Maybe if I got him drunk…

"I had the house almost completely rebuilt, got most of the roof done when I ran out of money. That's how I became a mail carrier.

"Did we miss lunch?"

My head was whirling as I stood. "I'll fix something."

Tanzy said she'd make coffee.

Then I heard the too close sound of the tractor. I pulled back the curtain to see Charles speeding up the driveway with Mickey in pursuit. Horrified, I saw the tractor leave the driveway and weave its unsteady path toward the veranda steps. Before I could exhale, Charles turned, and I watched him clip the old hitching post that stood beside the barn, then come to a lurching stop.

Mickey rushed up, waving and pointing.

I sat back in my chair. Tanzy said, "I'll make lunch, relax. Mickey sure is Charles's guardian angel."

I could only nod weakly. When I could speak, I said, "It's a study in contrasts. Who would have guessed that they would have become such close friends? Their backgrounds are so different—one a retired bank president, the other a rambunctious Irishman who still retains his Gaelic brogue when he gets excited. Speaking of Mickey, surely you know that he's in love with you."

"Yes, but he seems willing to settle for friendship and, believe me, that's not what I have in mind. I think he feels intimidated by the difference in our height. And I think he might be afraid of rejection—you know those Irish and their pride. I don't care about his height. He's shorter, but all man—man enough for me. They say good things come in small packages. I'd sure love to tear the wrapper off of that one. What's it going to take?"

Before Tanzy went home the next day, I said, "Don't forget your letter."

"Oh, toss it," she answered.

I glanced at the envelope quickly, then dropped it in the wastebasket.

The next morning, after the dishes were done, I sat down with the last cup of coffee. The house seemed empty. I dumped the coffee, rinsed the cup, and headed for the barn. I hadn't spent enough time with Ezzy these last busy weeks, and now, as I brushed her, she listened to my jumbled thoughts. I heard Charles's voice outside the closed barn door, then Mickey's laughter, and was thinking of joining them when I heard Tanzy's name. I stood back quietly and eavesdropped shamelessly.

"Mickey, that woman is in love with you."

"I doubt it. She just likes to kid around and bedevil me. But when I was young, I waved my money, what little I had, and drove to Portland every Wednesday and Saturday to see her dance. She was a stripper at the Golden Slipper burlesque theater, a fact not well-known around here. She was the star attraction and really packed them in—the place was always full. She danced for them, but she always came back to me—I swear she did—and danced only for me. I close my eyes and see her then. She was so beautiful—and still is. I see her leg around that pole and wish I was the pole."

With an embarrassed laugh, he added, "But then I was young and full of fire; now I'm old and only fourteen hands high and the fire has done gone out—old," he sighed.

"Old? That's just an excuse," said Charles, "and it isn't the size of the dog, but the size of the fight that's in that dog."

Their voices drifted away and I watched them walk toward that damn tractor.

That evening I asked Charles innocently, "What do you guys talk about all day?"

"Oh, this and that." He got comfortable in his chair and shook out the paper. I looked for my unfinished cookbook.

The silence was broken only by the rustle of the paper.

"Well, our little town is growing. It says here that a big land developer from Portland—J.W. Johnson—bought a big piece of land on the east side of town and plans to build tract homes."

Johnson, Johnson? Where had I seen that name before? The name tickled my memory.

Tanzy's letter!

In an instant the contents of the wastebasket scattered all over the kitchen floor. There it was, and stamped on the left corner of the envelope was "J.W. Johnson Land Developer, 740 NE Water Street, Portland, Oregon."

Wordlessly, I handed it to Charles.

When I was finally able to speak, I called Tanzy, my voice near frantic. "Oh, Emma, don't get too excited. I'll be over in the morning. Put the coffee on."

I didn't sleep all night.

Tanzy drove up in her battered old pickup about ten o'clock, blackberry vines still clinging to the tailgate. As usual when Tanzy was in the vicinity, Mickey showed up. We all sat at the table as I poured coffee.

Tanzy slowly opened the letter I had so urgently pressed into her hand. For a moment there was silence as she concentrated, then let out a shriek that challenged a high C as the letter flew into the air.

"What? What?" My voice was just below a scream.

"Johnson wants to buy my forty acres and is offering two thousand five hundred an acre. Of course, I'll keep ten acres, and now I can finish my house. Isn't that great?"

"How wonderful, Tanzy. We will celebrate!"

We hugged and cried as we danced around the kitchen. The men laughed at us, but their faces couldn't hide their pleasure.

Tanzy dropped my hand and picked up the letter. "Maybe I should read the rest of this. Okay, this says that Johnson plans to build some country estates and a shopping center, says my river frontage is beautiful. Uh-oh, this changes the picture. He says he has already bought the adjoining forty acres—that would be the Grieb place."

She walked to the window and stared out. It was obvious she wasn't admiring the landscape. When she turned there was a smile on her face, and I instinctively knew that Mr. Johnson was in trouble.

"He's looking forward to meeting me this Tuesday at one o'clock. Oh yes, we will need to do that—he doesn't know about the expensive easement he is going to buy at a reasonable cost, which I figure is about three hundred thousand dollars. Unless he makes me nervous, then the price will go up."

"Tanzy," Charles said, "What easement? You're way out here in the country."

"Well, the original owner was from Boston. He bought the land sight unseen and discovered when he arrived that his forty acres had no way in or out. Dad was sorry for him and together they put in that easement across our land. They did it with a horse-drawn plow and a shovel. There was no record because there were no escrow companies fifty or sixty years ago. Dad considered it a favor done. Now that favor will keep me a lot longer than two weeks. Yes, three hundred thousand should do it in the style I'll become accustomed to."

We listened almost spellbound.

"Perhaps I'll even let him build me a big house and deduct it from his obligation."

"Today," she emphasized, "he has no access to his forty-acre investment. Next Tuesday when I bring this to his attention, I'm sure he will be happy and make every effort to cooperate." She smiled that smile.

"Do you really think so, Tanzy?" I asked when I could talk.

"Of course. If he doesn't, I'll borrow Charles's tractor, and plow that easement up in two hours and plant corn."

Charles shook his head. "Tanzy, I don't wonder why you remind me of Mickey's dealing at the donkey races. You are two of a kind and you deserve each other."

"That's what I keep telling him," Tanzy laughed.

I wasn't surprised when the deal closed, exactly as she had said it would.

I spent time in the barn with Ezzy who would always meet me at the door. I wondered how she knew it was me. She would follow me back to her stall that was kept bedded in straw with a manger bulging with hay that she only nibbled at. Obviously her appetite was off. Then, too, she was lying down a lot and had difficulty getting to her feet. She was growing older before my eyes despite all the care and my daily visits.

I took my concerns to Mickey.

"Missus Halstad," he said, "we all grow older each day and someday we are going to our reward. You love that donkey so surely you won't regret her travelin' to another place where the grass is always green and knowin' she waits for you there."

I was comforted but heartbroken too.

Very early one morning the sun was barely up but I couldn't sleep. I pulled the covers snugly over Charles and hurried to the barn. After Ezzy met me at the door, I followed her frail steps back to the stall.

When she knelt on her knees, her back legs collapsed beneath her and she went down, her head in my lap, my arms around her for a last good-bye.

Through my tears I visualized her big head held high, tail flying, playing in a field where the grass was always green, and I was comforted.

This is where Mickey found me, the tears still damp on my cheeks in the first rays of the sun.

CHAPTER 15

A week later Tanzy drove up the driveway. This time I didn't smell the exhaust or hear the rattle of her old pickup. Instead came the quiet hum of a shiny red truck that obviously had yet to make the acquaintance of blackberry bushes.

"Where is Mickey?" she demanded. "It's been a week, and that blackberry patch is still where it was. It's going to be a hot day and he should have gotten an early start."

"Tanzy, you've got money enough to hire a crew. Why Mickey?"

Her voice grew soft. "I miss him. I just like to know he's there."

Pointing to the barn, I said, "He's probably in the barn doing Birthday Girl's hooves."

Then she was gone. So was Mickey.

Mickey didn't come home that night or the next. "Poor Mickey," I said. "She has worked him to death in that blackberry patch—that's where she is having the new house built."

"If Mickey would stop dragging his feet, he could live in that big house," Charles chuckled, then went back to his paper.

Breakfast was barely over the next morning when the truck came roaring up the drive with Mickey at the wheel. Charles pulled the curtain back and laughed. "Look at Mickey—he's absolutely swaggering. And look—he's got Tanzy by the hand."

We met them at the top of the steps.

"Mickey, where have you been? What's happening?"

"What's happening? A priest is what happened. Today. This very day we've been to the priest, we have," he said, grabbing Tanzy about the waist and whirling her around and around.

"Put me down," she laughed. "You Irish procrastinator, you."

As her feet touched the ground, I saw tears in her eyes.

"We'll have a real wedding right there in the church," Mickey exulted.

"I'll wear a dress," Tanzy added.

"A white one?" I teased.

"Of course," she answered.

And it happened exactly as she said.

The wedding was beautiful. True to her promise, Tanzy wore a long white dress with just a hint of a train, flowers in her hair, and a large bouquet of white and pink roses clutched in her hands.

"I've waited long enough for him," she said.

I was her maid of honor and Charles was the best man.

Mickey stood proudly beside her, stiff in his tuxedo, oblivious to the difference in height, a smile crossing his face from ear to ear.

Long and eloquent were the nuptials that proclaimed them man and wife.

Tanzy's make-up—and mine too—was streaked with tears. The men dabbed at their faces, Charles with his always immaculate white handkerchief.

Oh, my, the reception! Charles's wedding present was the out-of-town orchestra that played until dawn.

Hordes of friends were there; everybody loved Mickey and Tanzy.

"Where's the honeymoon, Mickey?" someone asked.

"Hell, we've had the honeymoon and it's gonna last forever," Mickey laughed.

It was the party to end all parties and the talk of the neighborhood for months.

Three weeks later, with the festivities over, Mickey came over to help Charles with the tractor—something about spark plugs and misfiring.

Hours later I heard their voices and the scrape of Mickey's chair on the veranda as he sat down. Charles came in. "I hope we have a six-pack in that fridge—that's about as long as this is going to take," he smiled. So saying, he departed with the beer.

I fought the urge to open that window, ashamed to be an eavesdropper, but some unearthly power took control and the window slid open noiselessly.

I heard the pop of the cans and their laughter, then Charles's voice. "Well, my friend, not so long ago you were too old, too short, and a confirmed bachelor. Now suddenly you're a happily married man. What happened?"

"It was an ambush, it was. That day she came and got me, I told her I was not going to chop any more of those hellish bushes down. She held me by my sleeve, she did, and begged, 'Just this last patch and I'll never ask you again. I'll even bring you down some beer.'"

It was quiet for a while, then Charles asked, "Well, what happened?"

"Well, I had cut me way in; had a narrow path where the vines had fallen. It was so damn hot, me shirt stuck to me back and it seemed to me as I worked my way in that those thorns got longer and sharper and snagged me at every step. I wiped the sweat from my eyes, and a vine, as though it was possessed by the divil himself, reached up and grabbed me by the foot. I fell like a brick. I kicked and kicked to free myself but the vines only curled tighter. I struggled to reach me clippers that had fallen just beyond me reach. Then the vines got me hand and I struggled until I was too tired and almost cooked to death in that hot sun. I just lay there and prayed to all the saints for Tanzy to come with the beer she promised. And she did."

"Mickey, that must have been horrible," Charles said.

Mickey laughed. "Well, yes and no. Tanzy looked down at me and said, 'So here you are, you lazy Irishman! Sleeping in the sun. And I was going to pay you double time to cut back just a few blackberry vines. Where are your clippers? Get up and get to work!'

" 'I sure as hell would if I wasn't tied down like a rodeo calf,' I told her. 'Did you bring the beer? I'm parched. Me clippers are just out of reach—see if you can get them. I'm helpless.'

"She laughed like a hyena, she did. 'You really are helpless,' she said, and crawled up the length of me to hold the beer to my lips. The thorns were stabbing me in the back and I groaned, 'Tanzy, for the sake of me sainted mother, cut me loose.'

"She was on top of me, wriggling around like a viper, sliding up and down. Said she was trying to reach the clippers. The sweat was about to drown me and I could feel—oh, how I could feel—and she just kept moving.

" 'Tanzy, Tanzy, I'm begging you. Cut me loose. What's it gonna take?' "

" 'I thought you'd never ask,' she said as she covered me like the plague, she did."

I moved closer yet to the window; wild horses couldn't have pulled me away.

"She was sweating too. I could taste it when she licked my lips. 'The beer,' she said, 'you've dribbled.' Then she added, 'Oh Mickey, you poor man, you must have injured yourself when you fell—there's a big bump here.'

"I felt her hands and they weren't on my belt buckle. Pretty soon I never noticed the thorns nor would I have noticed if I had been on a bed of nails. I've never envied that pole again—I was the pole and, Charles, there was no complainin' about the size of the fight!"

I heard Charles laugh louder than Mickey and was shocked at my refined husband.

Mickey asked if there was another can, and I heard the rattle of the empties. Then he said, "Later she still sat sidesaddle and said, 'Mickey, you conniving Irisher. Now that you've had your way with me, you're going to do the right thing, aren't you?'

"Again?

" 'Again and again,' she said, and so we did. Right there in the blackberry bushes. May they never die."

I was horrified. Right there in the bushes?

And they laughed—my Charles laughed. I almost closed the window.

When the laughter quieted down, Mickey went on. "I asked her if she was going to cut me loose now and she said, 'Tell me you love me.' I got all choked up when I told her, 'Ah, me darlin', you know I've always loved you and I always will.'

" 'What's the first, the very first thing you're going to do when I cut these vines?' She held up the clippers.

" 'Pull up me drawers and find the priest.' That's when she cut me loose."

I heard the truck leave and Charles brought in the empties.

One Sunday, the real winter with the cold rain arrived. The four of us were sitting around the table sated with the rich goodness of pot roast, but still finding room for apple pie.

"I wish we could go someplace where the flowers are blooming and it's warm," Tanzy said.

Then I thought of the last day of the cruise that Charles and I had so enjoyed. He had said then that the next cruise would be my choice. I had chosen the Greek Isles, the Golden Isles.

"Tanzy, you and Mickey never had a honeymoon. Why don't we all go on a cruise to the Greek Isles?" I enthused. "It's warm and beautiful there, and we'd have such a wonderful time."

"Of course. Mickey, let's have a honeymoon," Tanzy said as though it were just another cup of coffee.

Mickey looked a little dazed, but then rallied. "Of course, me darlin'."

And the cruise was booked.

It wasn't long before we found ourselves far out to sea strolling on a secluded deck in the moonlight, with Mickey and Tanzy behind.

With Charles's arm around me, he spoke, "Oh, Emma, this is so wonderful. We'll do it again."

I heard Mickey's snort of laughter and, in the soft darkness, I could feel Tanzy's smile.

Leaning closer, I whispered, "Oh, yes, again and again."

CHAPTER 16

Our ten days in paradise was an unforgettable memory. Reluctantly, we went home to the farm.

After a while, Charles grew tired of the "good-natured" advice that he endured day after day. "Charles, Charles! You're confused. That's the wrong end of the pitchfork." Or "That isn't a cow, Charles. That's not an udder."

Everyone else, including me, thought it was funny.

Finally, the laughter became unbearable to Charles, who retreated to the big house to brood over imaginary criticisms. As he sulked, the anger flourished; the house grew dark and cold.

In Charles's mind, anything that Mickey did was perfect. Anything that he did was ridiculed by me and Mickey and had to be redone and, of course, ridiculed. Finally Charles exploded with such a killing rage he even scared himself.

Yet again, Charles sat at the window and watched as Mickey manipulated that hellish machine with such confidence. They looked as if they had been cast from the same mold.

Charles's anger seethed and grew steadily as he watched. He saw his wife as being entirely too attentive to Mickey's every need. Mickey received her constant efforts with a familiar smile and a soft "thank you."

Hell's fire! Charles thought. Does Mickey need two women to take care of him? Tanzy seems oblivious to what is going on right under her nose. And Emma! Am I oblivious too? The way Mickey swaggers about, those black curls seeming to dance on his head, those flirty eyes never missing a thing—especially if hidden under a skirt!

Oh, oh, *oh*, Charles thought, if I could only catch him at it, I'd shoot him like the dog that he is. But I have to "play nice." His time will come, though. I'll watch him die if I can find my gun. Damn! Will you look at that! He and Emma, right in front of the barn! I think he wants to show me he can fondle my wife as easily as he can handle my tractor. I'll kill the bastard when I can find that damn gun.

Suddenly finding himself outside, with a voice thick with anger, Charles demanded, "Hold on there, Irishman. I want a word with you. Could you spare me a few minutes of your valuable time?"

"Of course, Charles. How can I be of help?" Mickey asked.

"You certainly can be of help. I would greatly appreciate it if you would cease your romantic attentions on my wife. Isn't Tanzy enough for you? Or is she too much for the so-called Great McNeil—the great womanizer?

"I'm going to talk to Emma too. We may as well include Tanzy in this little party—I've heard it's always the wife who's the last one to know. It will be the last party, I assure you. That I promise. You're done here—go home and start packing. As of now. Right now!

"I'm the head honcho here, which you seem to have forgotten, you dumb Irisher. In your spare time, maybe you can attend to your own wife. Quiet! I don't want any of your pitiful excuses, you stupid Irishman. Go home!"

"Charles! Have you lost your mind? Me 'n Emma? You must be crazy! She is like a sister to me. Surely you must know that she loves you like I love Tanzy—with all our hearts. We'd never stray. Get a grip! Back up! If I didn't hold you in such high regard, I'd have you on the ground begging! Shame on you!"

"Out! Out! Stay away from my wife or I'll shoot you on sight!"

Tears of rage covered the face of the man who stumbled home to Tanzy.

Speechless with shock, Mickey turned and left, passing me by on the porch as I held my basket filled with the canned peaches that Charles loved. That Mickey, I thought. Not even a hello. What is his big hurry, for goodness sake? Well, I'm so tired—walking to and from the market is so much exercise. And this basket weighs a ton.

I heaved a great sigh of relief as I set down the heavy basket and wiped away the sweat from my face with a coat sleeve.

CHAPTER 17

I hesitated at the doorway. The house seemed too quiet.

"Charles? I'm home, love, and glad to be here. Did you miss me like I missed you?"

In a voice I'd never heard before, Charles answered, "Emma, come here and sit down. Now! I intend to have a talk with you."

"Just a moment, love. I'll put the kettle on and we'll have a spot of tea. I'm exhausted…"

"Emma! I said come here. I won't say it again!"

Surprised and confused by his angry tone, I stepped in quickly, pushing the basket out of the way, and sat in the nearest chair. I looked up at the face of a Charles I'd never seen before and heard these unbelievable words that destroyed my world.

"I want to be the first to tell you that your lover is gone. I've just given him his walking papers. If I had my gun, I would have shot that wife-stealing Irishman.

"Emma, my cheating wife—and with the hired help yet and in the barn! How romantic! I've been watching you two. Do you think I'm stupid or blind? Only this morning I saw you plainly, wrapped up in his arms, right in front of the barn. Have you no shame? Poor Tanzy, your best friend! Her husband's a much better friend, right? Well, there will be no more of that. He has his walking papers as of right now. Poor Tanzy!

"I'll tend to this farm better than he ever could. I'll move those irrigation pipes with that big tractor—a job he was supposed to do last week. And I'll get back at you, my scheming, cheating wife, you may be sure. I'll have my eyes on you."

I had tried in vain to interrupt his tirade.

"You know that Ezzy died. And I was only crying on Mickey's shoulder. You know how he loves Tanzy—as I love you. Till death do us part. How can you say such terrible things? How can you?"

I sank back. My world shattered as I heard his ugly words. Words that smothered the happiness that had been mine. Was it only yesterday?

"Aha!" Charles dangled keys before my eyes. "You'll see. I can handle that tractor as well as that Irish womanizer—or better! Just watch!"

He was out the door, ignoring my tears, deaf to my pleas. I called Tanzy and heard Mickey's growl in the background, "Hell, he's just got to prove he's a farmer…"

I watched through the kitchen window as Charles hurried to the tractor shed where the big machine stood as if waiting for him. With horrified eyes, I saw the nose and heard the whine of that machine as it nudged its way to freedom. Charles blew me a defiant kiss as he began his dangerous trip with the forklift.

Instantly I was on my way, stepping in Charles's footsteps that showed plainly in the wet ground. As I reached my destination breathlessly, it was with a feeling of great relief when I heard the truck and saw Mickey at the wheel with Tanzy at his side.

We watched Charles speeding with a heavy load of pipes on the tractor. Even I could see how unevenly the pipes were stacked. Charles waved triumphantly.

"Dammit," Mickey growled. "I told him I was coming over today to pick up that pipe, but he had to go and play farmer."

A neighbor suddenly appeared and approached Mickey angrily.

"McNeil! Are you crazy? What the hell is going on here? Running that heavy machine on this wet hillside?!"

Mickey's face flushed and the neighbor stepped back quickly at Mickey's response.

The big tractor sped up, slipping and sliding with its heavy load of pipes, then turned sharply and headed down the hill, accelerating with every turn of the wheel. I knew Charles's foot was on the gas, knew he had confused the accelerator with the brakes, again. He was heading straight for my old barn.

Frantic, I shouted, "Slow down, Charles! Slow down! You'll kill yourself!"

Then my heart stopped. "Jump, Charles, jump!" I screamed, just as the tractor made a direct hit and his body flew through the air. I heard the loud splintering crash. Irrigation pipe, broken wood in every size scattered everywhere. The old barn tilted drunkenly. I could see daylight where I had never seen it before.

Charles lay prone beneath the tractor that was balancing on its back with three wheels and the stub of the fourth pointing heavenward as if begging forgiveness for the escapee rolling down the hill.

Helpless, I saw Charles desperately trying to free his arm from the sleeve held captive by the dark underparts of the big machine. I knew it would soon be dark. How are we going to free him?

I felt Tanzy's arms around me and heard Mickey's anguished cry, "No! No, please, God!" My eyes followed his pointing finger to the bloody gash in Charles's head.

Without a moment's hesitation, Mickey tore off his shirt, threw it over his shoulder, and began to crawl toward Charles. The neighbor reappeared and screamed, "Stop! Are you crazy? A breath of air will bring that hellish machine down. We'll have to dig you up to bury you—if there's anything left to bury."

Mickey didn't answer and didn't stop.

The neighbor turned helpless to Tanzy. "Tell him, missus. Talk to him! Can't you stop him?"

Instead, Tanzy called to Mickey, "I'm with you all the way, my darling. You can do it!"

Tanzy and I watched and prayed as Mickey made his slow, determined way to Charles. We were numb with fear as we saw him try to extricate his pocketknife from a darkness that held it captive. Just as it seemed hopeless, the knife slipped free. We breathed again as he sawed through the deadly snare.

Charles groaned as Mickey freed him to reveal a very nasty-looking leg, already starting to turn yellow at the knee and thigh. The movement also showed the source of the copious amount of blood that gushed from a large gash in his skull, pooling red on the wet black soil. Other than being momentarily stunned when he struck the ground, these seemed to be his only injuries.

"He's damn lucky," Mickey said. "Very damn lucky. Let's get him home and in bed."

With the neighbor's help, we managed to lift Charles into the bed of the truck, and the trip that seemed endless began. I knelt beside him and held his head that was wrapped in Mickey's shirt to cushion it from the bumps that Mickey couldn't avoid.

Home at last, we put Charles into bed, clean and warm with an icepack on his knee, his scalp cleansed and bandaged.

I called the doctor, who declined to visit until morning, but comforted me with the words, "Sounds like a superficial scalp wound and a badly sprained leg. I'll see you in the morning."

As Mickey prepared to leave, Charles's weak but determined voice was heard. "Mickey. Mr. McNeil. Please give me a moment. I want to tell you that I know I am alive because of your decency. I am living to plead—to beg!—for your forgiveness. And I do beg. Forgive me—for my incredible stupidity, my ignorance. And thank you for my life."

"No need to beg, Charles. Of course I forgive you for a few mischosen words spoken in a fever. I love both you and Emma. We are family, my brother you are, the Book says."

Tears glistened on the cheeks of both men as they embraced.

"You are a better man than I am, Gunga Din," said Charles.

CHAPTER 18

I cried as I changed the dressing on his head.

"Don't worry, Emma. It isn't broken. Just a little dent. Don't fuss so—it will get better. Is there any Tylenol?" he groaned.

I could feel the pain as though it were my own. I cried as I discarded Mickey's lifesaving contribution—his work shirt—that wrapped around Charles's head and stopped the pulsing flow of blood. Tylenol and ice packs didn't seem to help, although I kept them coming. Charles was sweating, trying not to groan. I was trying to keep my composure and the ice packs refreshed.

"How is he doing?" Mickey asked.

Charles's sweaty face and his muffled groans told Mickey without words as Charles vainly tried to get comfortable. With effort, Charles said, "Emma, do we have any of that medicinal orange juice in the house?"

"I'll fix it, I will! I know where the vodka is!" exclaimed Mickey.

He returned very shortly with four glasses on a tray, accompanied by a big pitcher, the contents of which were almost colorless.

The first drink helped soothe Charles, and I was weak with relief. Three more glasses of medicinal orange juice and Charles was sleeping peacefully. I was very drowsy. The ice bag had melted, and the big pitcher was empty.

When Mickey and Tanzy showed themselves out, I noticed Tanzy seemed somewhat unsteady.

The mental strain and physical effort had taken their toll on me too. I was very tired, so I donned my nightgown and slipped into bed, disregarding the clock that showed only eight o'clock.

As I cuddled against Charles's back and listened to the falling rain as it spattered against the roof, the memories of the past year flooded my consciousness.

This love, so freely given. This love may falter for a moment, but it will never die. Our deep, enduring friendship with Mickey and Tanzy. This was my life after so many years alone. This unexpected new life! I had thought my remaining time was enough, but now this joy made me know for the first time that I was truly alive.

My life had not been done; it had just been on hold, waiting in the wings for Charles.

He turned, his loving arm pulling me closer until my head rested on his shoulder, and whispered the words that made me want to live forever. "I love you, and I know you love me."

I cuddled closer still, closed my eyes, said my prayers.

Sleep crept in on tiny cat feet, and I knew.

Tomorrow is forever.

ABOUT THE AUTHOR

Dolores Durando, born in 1921, is the author of *The Long Journey Home, And Yesterday is Gone, Beyond the Bougainvillea, Out of the Darkness, Always in the Ribbons,* and *Tomorrow is Forever.* Dolores gained deep intuition for the diversity of human nature as a licensed psychiatric technician for more than forty years in various mental hospitals. She served on mental health advisory boards, both in California and Oregon, with fourteen years as a board member of *ASSET,* a nationally published magazine, for which she wrote short stories. She retired at seventy and moved to Oregon, where she has been writing, painting watercolors, and sculpting. She lives with her son and daughter-in-law in southern Oregon's stunning Applegate Valley.